FROST BITE

Nelson Brunanski

Caronel Publishing

Victoria Canada

Copyright 2010-01-21

Library and Archives Canada Cataloguing in Publication

Brunanski, Nelson, 1950-
Frost Bite : another small-town Saskatchewan mystery /
Nelson Brunanski.

ISBN 978-0-9739121-1-1

I. Title.

PS8603.R85F76 2009   C813'.6   C2009-903783-1

Caronel Publishing
Victoria Canada

Cover Art and Design: Gerry Mayer & Monir Shahir
Typesetting: Nelson Brunanski
Printed and Bound in Canada

This book is dedicated to
all those who encourage and/or
inspire me to write

Including: Ed and Jean Brunanski, Carole Clement, Trent and Noel Brunanski, Craig Brunanski, Paul Grescoe, Steve Scriver, Jen and Brett Howie, Jenny Young, Donald Gessner, Gerry Mayer, Lynn Wittenberg and Doug Thordarson, Wendy Lum and Bernie Neufeld, Lynn Fern and Rene Beauchamp, Mary Norek, the Waldbilligs, Clements, Glazers, Noreks, Lamendas, Molnars, Redheads and Mitchells, Dean and Cheryl Hildebrandt, Anthea Penne, Kay McCracken, Deanna Kawatski, David and Debbie Dagoli, Mike Garnett and Maureen, Dave and Shirley Barret, Harry and Bernadette Klassen, Maidra Cresswell, Georges Payrastre and Claudine Viallon, Garth and Sabine Reimer, MaryAnn Simmons, Susan Woods and Greg Evans, Sid Tafler, Robyn Bryson, Linda Foubister, Marianne Kimmitt and Bill Rowe, Marlin and Sybille Wilson, Carolyn Bateman, Neale Donald Walsch, Mary and Austin Hennessey, Sandra at Absolutely Books, Sandra Swift at APG Books, Wakaw Recorder, Wakaw Pharmacy, The Crossroads, Wakaw Public Library, town of Wakaw, province of Saskatchewan, all the folks who read Crooked Lake and/or Frost Bite, and to all of those who I missed, a special thank you.

I'm standing in front of the Wheat Pool grain elevator with Corporal Fred Snell, head of the Crooked Lake RCMP detachment. The detectives we've been waiting for arrive in a low-slung, black station wagon. I recognize Sergeant Hutt as he hoists himself out of the deep passenger seat. He pulls a pack of du Mauriers out of his jacket pocket and lights up. "Hello, Bart," he says to me. His smoky scowl suggests he's not happy to be back in Crooked Lake.

"So, what have we got in there, Fred?" Hutt jerks his head in the direction of the elevator.

"From what I could see it's a body buried under a pile of wheat. But I didn't go inside." Fred explains that he didn't want to contaminate the scene any more than I already had.

"What did you see?" Hutt turns to me.

"Same thing, a body under a pile of wheat."

"Did you touch anything?"

"There was a hand sticking out," I say, "so I felt for a pulse."

"And?"

"There was none. In fact his hand felt stiff, like it was frozen or something."

"Frozen?" Hutt's partner Detective Klassen says. "It's fifty friggin' degrees outside, Bartowski."

He doesn't need to remind me. I shrug my shoulders and zip up my jacket against the cool September evening.

"Now," Hutt's voice is as flat as the prairie, "what were you doing here?"

I gaze toward the lake a quarter mile away but can feel Hutt's eyes watching me. "I was just driving by, saw the car there." A shiny, new Lincoln Town Car sits in front of the elevator. "The driver's door was hanging open, dinging."

"So?"

"So, I shut the door."

Both detectives frown forebodingly. Last spring Hutt and Klassen investigated what turned out to be a double homicide in Crooked Lake. I think I rubbed them the wrong way when I got mixed up in the thing.

"What time did you find the body?" Klassen says.

"Seven-thirty-two."

"How can you be so sure?"

"That's what it said on his watch."

Klassen gives me a *don't get smart* look.

A police van marked *forensics* pulls up next to the detectives' wagon. A few minutes later two officers wearing gloves, white coveralls and paper hats, each loaded down with gear, climb the ramp into the elevator. Soon the dark interior of the building is lit up by dozens of flashes.

Before long the schiff-whiff of an aluminum shovel echoes from the cavernous building—the corpse being exhumed from its grainy tomb. Fred Snell, who's been watching over the scene, beckons with a wave and Hutt and Klassen ascend the ramp into the elevator.

Ray Chow, the local doctor, who acts as the town's coroner arrives to carry out his duty, which he once told me is to declare the victim deceased, unless of course he isn't. He looks a little rattled when he comes out of the elevator a few minutes later. He gives me a sober nod before putting his black bag into his small SUV and driving away.

Fred ushers me over to his police cruiser. "We need to get a handle on this before it gets out, Bart, so don't go blabbing about it with anybody, and that includes Rosie." He waves a long bony finger at me.

A few minutes later, glowering, Sergeant Hutt emerges from the elevator and trundles down the truck ramp. "You know this guy?" he asks, handing me a polaroid picture.

I examine it closely.

Hutt's glower deepens. "Well, do you?"

One Week Earlier
Stuart Lake Lodge
Northern Saskatchewan

———————

"I'm your host, Bart Bartowski," I say, steadying the tall, lean, fiftyish man who steps down from the floatplane onto the dock.

"I'm Lionel Morrison," he replies. His handshake is firm and dry, though his complexion is a little green.

Al, the pilot of the twin otter, reported hitting some nasty weather out of the northeast. That might account for the green pallor.

Still, Morrison says, gamely, "We've heard good things about your lodge, Bart."

"Glad to hear it," I say. And I am, because Lionel Morrison is no less than the CEO of Sombrero, a multinational agra-corporation. He and seven other execs are here for a week of fishing.

With the aircraft unloaded, hands shaken and names exchanged, I take our guests up the winding, tree-lined boardwalk to their cabins while Rosie puts the finishing touches to lunch.

Morrison's complexion gains some colour as he breathes deeply and takes in the view from the cabin's deck. The sun is hitting the lake and reflecting into his expressive brown eyes. They light up as he hears the rushing water of a rapid a few hundred yards off.

"This is surely God's country," Morrison says, almost to himself.

After showing them where things are in the two bedroom cabin I leave them to settle in.

Jack Kolchak, a good-looking fellow with thick dark hair and quick eyes, is the first to arrive at the main lodge for lunch. He's followed by Lionel Morrison and his burly buddy who calls himself Chas. A fire is warming up the lodge after near freezing over-night temperatures. September nights can get real chilly this far north.

Our head guide Charlie Mackenzie sits on a couch near the fireplace sipping from a stainless steel travel mug. His grizzled braids hang down the back of his thick, well-worn Siwash sweater. He slides over when Jack Kolchak sits down a little too near him.

Elbows on his knees, head slung toward Charlie, Kolchak says, "How's the fishing?"

"It's good," Charlie says, his heavily wrinkled face expressing good cheer. Charlie's family has run trap lines and kept a summer camp up here for generations, so he knows when the fishing is good.

"It better be," Kolchak says, "because I told them I'd be bringing back a trophy lake trout to hang in my office."

Charlie's eyes widen a bit.

"Next to my marlin."

Charlie's eyes widen a bit more.

Having overheard, I take a seat across from Kolchak. "I'm afraid folks back at your office are going to be disappointed then," I say.

"Why? You saying I can't catch a trophy fish?"

"No, I'm saying it's all catch and release here."

"What do you mean?"

"Well, just that."

"Not even a trophy fish?" he says, his voice incredulous.

I twist my head apologetically.

"Do you hear this?" he spits in the direction of Lionel Morrison and Chas who have taken seats near by.

"We can take pictures," Lionel suggests.

"I brought my digital," another new arrival offers.

Kolchak rolls his eyes. "Great. I'll paste a *picture* of a fish next to my marlin."

"Come and get it boys," Rosie sings out, bringing the charged moment to an end. The men obediently make their way to a buffet table laden with oven-warm baking, freshly-caught trout with bacon and eggs, toast and coffee. Rosie has even managed a fruit salad despite this being the last of a month-long stint at the lodge. She goes around filling coffee cups and chatting with the men. She always draws a crowd. Her long blond hair and good figure probably have something to do with it.

After everyone is settled in, Chas says, "Mr. Morrison don't eat wheat."

"I've got an allergy," Morrison explains, but don't worry about me. There's plenty here to eat." His complexion has turned from green to grey. Neither colour very healthy looking.

But always Johnny-on-the-spot, Rosie rounds up some cornmeal muffins that she baked earlier for shore lunch. The men eat with good appetites, enthusing over the taste and texture of the fresh trout.

After lunch four motorboats roar away from the dock, each carrying two fishermen and a guide. At the mouth of the deep bay the four boats will separate into two parties, each exploring a different part of the long leggy lake.

"So what do you think of the gang so far?" I say, sipping hot black tea. Rosie and I have attended to our various chores, her prepping for supper, including the prime rib roast, me mending the electric fence so it will last through the long hard winter.

"They're nice," Rosie says. "Especially Lionel. He's so friendly. Then there's that young buck."

"Who? Kolchak? Why do you call him that?"

"I don't know. He's younger and more aggressive than the rest . . . and he's quite a hunk."

"A hunk, eh?"

"Well, he's one hell of a good looking man." Rosie shoots out a hip.

"Rosie," I protest.

"Well . . . I can't help that, can I?"

She's right, of course, though he's a little too cute for my taste.

"I think he's after Morrison's job," Rosie says.

"Why do you say that?"

"He acts like he's in charge already."

I twist my lips and nod in concurrence.

Rosie doesn't usually respond to anyone in particular. Nor does she often describe anyone as a hunk, except me once in a while, though not as often as she used to.

After giving her a proprietary hug, I shamble up to the Sugar Shack for a short nap before the boats return. The shack was the first cabin we built, and gave us a place to live while the remainder of the lodge was under construction. We eventually built an addition, including an extra bedroom and an indoor toilet to accommodate the children and provide a modicum of civility for our seasonal stays. This brings to mind our youngest who is at home under the tutelage of Rosie's mom. I hope they're getting along okay. They're both pretty hard headed.

I wake to the familiar whine of distant outboard motors filtering through the trees. Butch and I meander down to the dock, timing our arrival with that of the first two boats. Four grinning, wind-burned faces look back at us. Even Kolchak has a smile on his face. Charlie looks at me as he guides the sixteen-foot aluminium boat gently to the dock. His face, as usual, is unreadable, making him a daunting poker player.

All appears well until I see lying in the bottom of Charlie's boat, a giant lake trout, its mouth agape, glassy eyes fixed.

Charlie points his puckered lips in Jack Kolchak's direction.

Kolchak looks at me defiantly as he climbs out of the boat. "Come on," he says, "tell me that's not a trophy fish."

"That will have to be the first and last fish that doesn't go back in the water or into a fry pan," I say, with as much authority as I can muster.

Kolchak stands back, keeping his eyes on the horizon. He gives away nothing.

"The reason we have fish that size is because we put them back and let them mature. Some of these trout live thirty or forty years."

After I finish my little speech, he says, "So, what do we do with it?"

I haven't dealt with a trophy fish for so long, it takes me a moment to remember how to prepare one for taxidermy. But of course I have no intention of mounting the fish. "Charlie, will you fillet that for me," I say.

"No way," Kolchak says.

Turning from his chores at the back of the boat, Charlie looks calmly at Kolchak and reaches for the twenty-five pound lake trout that lies in a pool of its own making. With a derisive snort, Jack Kolchak turns and heads toward his cabin.

The other set of boats appears. Lionel Morrison looks somewhat relieved as he climbs onto the dock.

Chas peers at me as if he's about to tell me my dog died. "Mr. Morrison needs a rest, see," he says, sounding like Rocky one, two and three.

"Sure," I say, not wanting to mess with the muscled hulk.

"He can only take so much, you know what I'm saying."

"I know what you're saying," I say, not knowing what he's saying. But Chas adds nothing more.

Morrison overhears the last exchange. "Don't worry about me," he says, but he looks worn out. "My allergies are giving me a few problems, that's all."

"We have a little delay in supper, so we'll eat about seven, if that's okay?"

"Suits me," Morrison says, looking at his watch. "'Course I don't know what time it is anyway, there are so many dials on this thing."

By way of a smile Chas bares his teeth, displaying a mouth full of gold fillings, then he and Lionel Morrison slowly climb the boardwalk.

At seven the men begin to arrive at the lodge for supper. Morrison and Chas join a couple of others at a table overlooking the lake. The sunset has turned the opposite shore ablaze in fall colours. The crimson and gold of poplar and birch mingle with the evergreens. The men drink cocktails and trade stories about the big one that got away, except for Jack Kolchak who complains about the big one that didn't get away.

"That was one hell of a fish," he says. "Too bad I won't be taking it home in one goddamned piece." He goes on to explain to the others, with not a little disdain, why he won't be taking his prize catch home on a mounting board. The men at his table look uncomfortable, those at Lionel's avoid the discussion all together.

With no more misadventures, the group settles into a routine of fishing and fine food, followed by drinks and bullshit until lights out.

On the fifth and final day of the trip, the fishing boats head out again, but short two anglers. Lionel has decided to relax today and his constant companion Chas will do the same. Over a leisurely breakfast on the deck, we trade family stories. When I tell Morrison our daughter and son-in-law are both environmentalists, he can't hide his enthusiasm.

"We need to rein in our impact on the planet soon if we expect to survive," he says, "because even maintaining the status quo isn't good enough. But somebody's got to draw the line. The governments aren't doing it. We've been asking them for years to set guidelines, but they keep waffling, not willing to risk contributions or votes." I guess even CEOs are at the government's mercy. His eyes follow a v-shaped flock of Canada geese heading south, silent against the crisp blue sky.

"One thing that concerns me is this bio-fuel business," I say. "We have people starving to death in the world, yet we continue to feed our gas-guzzlers."

"I think we need to fine-tune the industry," Lionel says. "Ethanol uses the crop itself to create fuel. Bio-diesel, or biomass on the other hand is made from the non-edible parts of the plant. But they both have a very high carbon footprint for the amount of fuel they actually produce. Solar and wind are much more economical, especially in the prairies where you have plenty of both. But there are strong lobbies for ethanol within the company." I could imagine Kolchak among them. "From what I've seen, you've got a pretty green approach to things up here, Bart."

"All of our electricity is solar. We fly out our garbage and compost everything else. We try our best to co-exist. It works out most of the time." Though a bearskin rug lies on the floor in front of the fireplace, a victim of the inevitable conflict between man and nature.

"How'd you like to visit one of my favourite fishing spots?" I say, taking a genuine liking to the guy.

"Sure thing," Lionel says. Chas gives one of his teeth-baring grins. I can tell he's anxious to get out on the lake again. The feel of a fish on your line is like a drug. You quickly succumb to its lure.

We meet at the dock a half hour later. I've got the net, a six-pack and enough wheat-free snacks to keep us going well into the afternoon. The day could only be described as glorious. Sun reflects off the water, the aluminium boat and Chas's gold teeth.

On the way we make a stop at the McKenzie's summer camp to drop off some things Rosie sent along. The camp is on an island populated by Charlie's extended family. They have occupied what's come to be known as Mackenzie Island since the 1950s when they came seeking fresh trap lines and to escape the modernity of the town of La Ronge.

Dogs bark and children race to the dock to meet us. I guide the boat in, and a young boy of about twelve takes the rope and ties it off expertly. We are led to Charlie's shack tent that sits in a line of similar shelters—a permanent wooden frame is stretched tight with a seasonal canvas roof, leaving a hole for the metal chimney. The smell of wood smoke mixes with tanned leather and dog hair. Standing in her doorway, Marlene, Charlie's young wife, grins at us. Her twin baby boys are attached to her engorged breasts. Unabashed, she disengages them one at a time, much to their chagrin, handing one off to a girl of about nine or ten and the other, screaming loudly, to Marlene's mother, who wears a permanent grin. Or it may be her dentures.

We drink tea poured from a blackened kettle that resides on top of the airtight stove. While combing her long, black hair, Marlene tells us about how Charlie made a pile of money at the casino in Prince Albert last month.

"He's takin' us to Vegas," she says, and though it's

said in her usual monotone, the look in her eyes says her dreams might come true in Vegas. "We're gonna see Shania."

Several small children are milling about the hot stove. They manage to stay out of trouble for the most part.

"Charlie told me about the trophy fish," Marlene says. "We don't keep fish like that, usually. Unless we need food for the dogs." She puts another split log into the stove. "Charlie always says, let them fish go. If they lived this long, they earned the right. But sometimes we feed them to the dogs." She grins broadly, displaying a plug of chewing tobacco that is lodged behind her bottom teeth.

Accompanied by her brood, Marlene takes us on a tour of the encampment, with its icehouse, smoke shack and latrine, a two-holer, sheltered from the rain by a thick thatch of willow. We follow a narrow path that leads to a small lake at the centre of the island. The young boys that met our boat are now paddling a wooden canoe through a bed of wild rice, bending the stems and beating the heads, dislodging the black grains into the bottom of the boat. Both Lionel and Chas are fascinated by the scene.

Returning from the lake, we bid Marlene goodbye, but not before she unwraps a hide containing smoked trout—northern candy, we call it—and passing it around to everyone. I leave her the half-dozen litres of UHT milk and two family-size bags of Dad's cookies that Rosie sent. Soon the twins form a bleating chorus to get back to their interrupted suckles.

"I've never seen anything like this," Morrison says. "It's like going back in time."

Chas grunts his agreement.

The children come out to say goodbye, waving their cookies as we push off.

A half-hour boat ride to the south is my favourite fishing spot. It's a small sandy bay where you can easily spot northern pike, also known as jackfish, swimming against the white sand bottom. With his first cast, Lionel catches a fighting ten-pound northern pike, with his second a fifteen-pounder. He works the rod and reel seriously, but can't keep a grin off his face. He and Chas fish the bay for a couple of hours, catching probably twenty-five fish and releasing twenty-five.

"It doesn't get much better than this," Lionel says, with a deep satisfying exhalation. "We've got to protect the health of this planet if only so places like this can go on existing just as they are."

Like all giant multinationals, Sombrero is famous for its less than caring attitude toward the earth, yet here is Lionel Morrison, its CEO, talking like a flaming environmentalist.

As we stow our gear for the trip back to the lodge, a moose appears at the shoreline. It treads into the water, hooves stirring up the fine white sand. As the big animal bows to drink, a calf trots out of the bush on limber legs. Lionel fires off about twenty pictures before the cow and calf disappear into the thick bush once again.

"Unbelievable," Morrison says.

"Like you say," Chas agrees, in his Bronx accent.

"I can see why this is your favourite spot," Lionel says. "I'll send you copies when I get home," he adds, holding up his camera in a salute.

Later that afternoon the Sombrero guys load their gear onto the twin Otter. On the dock Rosie and I, Charlie and all the staff bid them farewell with handshakes and, in some cases, hugs. Some very large tips are passed around to guides and staff before the eight men climb aboard the plane that will transport them back to La Ronge. From there they will board their private jet for the flight to Saskatoon.

After cleaning up the cabins and the lodge with the help of Charlie's two nieces, Rosie and I and Butch climb aboard our Cessna 185 for the two and a half hour flight south to our home in Crooked Lake.

"Yeah, I know him," I say, examining the polaroid picture Sergeant Hutt has handed me.

"Who is he?" Hutt says.

"What happened to him?"

"All we want is for you to ID the guy," Klassen says.

The distinctive, multi-dialled watch that stuck out of the pile of wheat was a dead giveaway.

"His name is Lionel Morrison," I say, though the picture looks nothing like the Lionel Morrison I remember.

"How do you know him?"

"He was at my lodge fishing."

"Yeah?"

"With a group from Sombrero."

"Sombrero, eh?" Hutt bites his lower lip and writes in a coil-bound notebook. "What did he do for Sombrero?"

"CEO," I say.

"Jesus," Hutt says, raising his head, "you mean this guy's the christly chief executive officer of Sombrero Incorporated?"

"Yeah."

"They're going to love this back at headquarters," Klassen says, genuine excitement in his voice.

"Okay, let's start again," Hutt says, lighting another

cigarette. Smoke pours out of his mouth as he says, "These Sombrero guys were up at your lodge, when exactly?"

"Last week, arrived Monday mid-morning, and left Friday afternoon."

"And where are they from?"

"Morrison lived in Mexico City." Lionel told me they transferred their head office there for tax reasons. "As for the others, I can't say exactly where they lived. But there was one from Saskatoon." Kolchak had argued that Saskatoon was the new Chicago.

"Anybody else from the company in Crooked Lake?" Hutt asks.

"I don't know. I assume all those who came for the announcement have left."

"What announcement?" Hutt says.

"That's why Morrison was here, to announce the new Sombrero distribution terminal they plan to build north of town."

Hutt exchanges glances with Klassen. "Who else was here for that?"

"I don't know, except for Jack Kolchak, the one from Saskatoon and Morrison's body guard."

"Bodyguard?" Hutt looks up from his note taking.

"Actually he was referred to as his assistant. But when you meet him, you'll see what I mean. He was always with Morrison, never left his side."

"Except this time," Hutt says.

"Yeah, except this time."

"Okay, now tell me what you were really doing here?" he says. I'm not a very good liar.

I nod toward the elevator. "I was looking for him."

"You were looking for Lionel Morrison?"

"Yeah."

"So, you're trying to find a guy who is busy getting himself killed? Why were you trying to find him?"

"I invited him for supper."

"Oh," Klassen says, as though that explained everything.

"Yeah, I was going to barbecue steaks, so when he didn't show up I went looking for him."

"Why did you invite him for supper?" Klassen says.

"What do you mean?"

"Were you friends?" Klassen says. "Buddies?"

"No," I say. "What are you implying?"

"I just want to know why you invited the CEO of Sombrero to come to your house for supper. Is that too complicated for you?" Klassen says.

I exchange glances with Hutt, then say, "When I heard they were coming to Crooked Lake for the new Sombrero plant, I did the neighbourly thing and invited him for a barbecue. Besides, I liked the guy and wanted him to feel welcome." I shake my head. "Ironic, eh?"

Corporal Klassen looks at me as if he's just eaten something that's off. "What do you mean by ironic?" he says.

"Well," I say, "instead of feeling welcome, Lionel is dead. He couldn't be much less welcome than that, could he?"

"Yeah, ironic," Klassen says, as though only wimps would use the word.

"All right," Detective Hutt says. "You invited Morrison for supper. What time did you expect him?"

"Six-thirty."

"But he didn't show up?"

"Right."

"So?"

"So, I went to the motel."

"And?"

"He wasn't there."

"So?" Hutt makes a full body movement, like Archie Bunker begging Edith to get on with it.

"Chas tried to call Morrison on his cell phone," I say.

"What time was that?" Klassen says.

"Must have been seven-fifteen or thereabouts."

"Why wasn't his bodyguard with him?" Hutt says.

"He stayed at the motel to watch the baseball game on TV. The Yankees are playing for the pennant."

"So, he's watching baseball while his boss, the one he's supposed to protect, is getting himself killed?"

"Looks like," I say. Hutt and Klassen exchange glances.

A few minutes later Hutt leaves me standing there while he uses the wooden rail to pull himself up the stairs and back into the grain elevator. Klassen follows.

After some crackling on his shoulder radio, Fred says, "You can go now, Bart, but keep yourself available for further questioning. And remember what I said about blabbing."

"Sure, Fred," I say, getting into my truck, grateful to be out of the chilly night air.

When I arrive home, I take Rosie in my arms. She pulls back. "What's the matter?" she says. "Where've you been all this time?" Worry lines wrinkle her smooth skin.

"I found Lionel," I say.

"Where is he?" Her blue eyes are expectant.

"I found him under a pile of wheat at the Pool elevator."

She looks at me, a bewildered frown on her face.

"Honey, Lionel is dead." As I say the words, the whole thing becomes real for the first time, the man is actually dead. The man that we got to know and like, not as the CEO of Sombrero, but as a guy in khaki pants who talked fishing and retold jokes that his granddaughter had told him.

"Who's dead?" Our thirteen-year-old son's head pops over the railing of the loft.

I look at Rosie miserably and say, "You better come down, Stu."

"What's going on?" he says, coming down the loft stairs and taking a seat at the kitchen table where Rosie and I have settled next to each other.

"Lionel Morrison, one of our guests at the lodge is dead," I say.

"Wha'd he die of?" Stu says.

"We don't know yet."

"Where'd he die?" Stu looks from me to Rosie.

"At the Pool elevator."

"What was he doing there?"

"Stu, I don't know," I say. "That's enough questions for now. And I need you both to keep quiet about this too. The police don't want it spread around."

They both nod, vaguely.

"You okay, Mom?" Stu says to Rosie who gazes unhappily into her open palms that are resting in her lap.

Rosie looks up at him. "I'm fine," she says, reaching out and covering Stu's hand with her own.

"I'm starving," I say, getting up and opening the fridge. "Anybody else feel like a steak?"

By morning news of the murder has spread around the globe. And my name is always in the middle of it as *the guy who found the body.*

Even Dee Elliot, editor of the Crooked Lake *Reporter,* tries to get the goods. "Tell me about it," she says, when I run into her at the post office.

"There's nothing to tell."

"Come on, you found the body."

"And I was told not to talk about it with anybody."

"I'm not anybody, I'm the press."

I shake my head.

"This is big news," Dee says. "CEOs don't get murdered every day."

"I guess not."

"There's a lot of land being swallowed up by companies like Sombrero."

"I s'pose," I say.

"And that's making some people mad, maybe mad enough to do something like this."

The hairs on the back of my neck come to attention. "You think somebody's trying to make a point by killing the CEO of Sombrero?" I say.

"Exactly."

"Isn't that a little extreme?"

"And that's why it's an editor's dream," Dee says. "The CEO of Sombrero buried under a ton of wheat in Crooked Lake, Saskatchewan, breadbasket of the world? You gotta be kidding me?"

But it's no joke. Newspapers, network TV and wire services all show up in town. Lionel Morrison is described as an able corporate leader, and a generous man who, along with his wife, Margaret, directed a philanthropic organization aimed at those suffering from life-threatening allergies. Some of the networks played up Lionel's own struggle with allergies. It's thought that his health issues were exacerbated by his move to Mexico City. He was considered green as far as CEOs of agra companies go. Certain factions within the company had it in for Morrison, interested in profit, no matter the cost to the environment. I put Kolchak in that category.

"We're famous," Stuart declares when I get home. "It's on the internet. Your picture's everywhere. Cool, eh?"

"Yeah, cool," I say.

On the CNN website there are pictures of all the prominent players in Morrison's life and death, including the town itself, and yours truly, described as *hair black, eyes brown, 40 year's-old, six feet tall, 180 lbs.* The pictures of me are stolen off the lodge website, so I look quite sporty.

"Check out the new town site," Stuart says, "they got this sexy chick talking." He clicks the link to the Town of Crooked Lake website. As images of the town scroll by, a pleasant female voice narrates.

The town of Crooked Lake, Saskatchewan is home to approximately a thousand people, and is rapidly growing. The province's robust economy is generating unprecedented housing and business opportunities. A large RCMP detachment is based in Crooked Lake. A hospital and an excellent school, skating rink and recreation centre afford residents healthy, safe environs in which to learn and grow. One-hour access to Saskatoon, the hub of the province and the nearby lake from which the town derives its name are two of the key factors in Crooked Lake's sustainability.

Stu clicks back to the CNN site, but having seen enough, including too many shots of my own mug, I ask him, "What do you think?"

"Crooked Lake is on the map," he says.

"Not a great way to get on the map," I suggest.

He shrugs. "Famous or infamous. It's all the same these days."

"Which one are we?" I say.

"That has yet to be seen, doesn't it?" Stu says, as though this were a reality TV show and the outcome would only be revealed on the last episode.

I yell down to Rosie, "What's for dinner?"

"What are you making?" she yells back.

Not an atypical response. I head down to the kitchen.

The mid-day meal was the biggest of the day back when there were farms all across the land and people worked from sunup to sundown. Dinner it was called back then, and dinner it's called today. Except by corporate farmers who work eight to five and take a half-hour lunch break.

"It'll just be you and Stu," Rosie says. "The caterer is coming and Annie and I are trying out dishes for the reception."

"So, you're not making dinner, is that what you're saying?"

"You've got it, Watson," Rosie says. "Besides, I've been too busy with the wedding today to even think about cooking."

"They could have got married last fall," I say, "then all this would be unnecessary."

"You are such a jerk sometimes," Rosie says, briskly pulling her long blond hair into a ponytail. "Our only daughter and you want her wedding to be over and done with so you can spend your time loafing around." She snaps a rubber band around her hair.

"That's not fair," I say.

"I'm glad they postponed it," Rosie says. "Now we can have a proper wedding. One we can all be proud of."

Who's this wedding for, I wonder, Annie or us? I dare not say this aloud though. Instead I head over to the fridge. "Soup and sandwiches?" I shout to Stu up in the loft.

Our daughter Annie and her partner Randall arrived

a week ago from Iqualuit, Nunavut Territory. After a year up there, they decided it was just too remote for them and their nine-month-old baby, Emma. So, they're going to be staying with us for their wedding, and until Randall finds a new job, which I hope is soon. Happily there's a real demand for environmental scientists these days.

Rosie takes a seat at the dining room table and I watch as she goes through the long list she has in front of her, stroking some items off and adding others. Curious, I look over her shoulder. Next to liquor she writes: *Remind Bart.* She closes her folder, labelled in big block letters, *Wedding, September 29th.* Just ten days to go.

"Here's a picture of the cake," Annie says, bursting into the kitchen holding a magazine in one hand and baby Emma in the other. She takes a seat at the table. "Isn't it incredible? It has three tiers with the bride and groom descending a staircase of icing. And the best part is," she says in baby talk to Emma, "it's chocolate."

Which is appropriate since Annie and Randall met at a candy machine, both searching for change and chocolate while studying environmental studies at the U. of S.

"Which reminds me, where's your fiancé?" I ask.

"He's in Moose Jaw, helping his folks move."

Rosie's eyes find mine.

I raise my eyebrows in ignorance.

"I didn't know they were moving," Rosie says. "Did they buy a new house?"

"No, they're moving into an apartment."

"An apartment?" Rosie says, looking confused. "How come?"

"I don't know," Annie says. "Maybe they just wanted a change."

"How're they doing?" Rosie asks.

"Fine," Annie says, obviously tiring of the questions.

Ignoring Annie's tone, Rosie says, "I wonder how they'll get all their furniture into an apartment."

"Don't worry about it," Annie says in a manner suggesting she wants done with this topic. I give Rosie my meaningful look hoping she'll get the hint. She gives me an annoyed look back, but relents.

Annie shows us a picture of the dress she's chosen for the going away outfit. Traditionally the bride and groom leave the wedding reception early to ensure their presence never gets stale. They return, but only briefly, in their *going away outfits* to say their final goodbyes. The less formal attire is just right to take them on the usually short car trip to their marriage boudoir.

The dress is in fact a black pinstriped suit with a short jacket and equally short skirt. The model looks sexy in it. I wonder if Annie will look sexy in it too. I hope not for some reason. I still imagine her as a little girl, pug nosed and curly haired, chasing around the kitchen table and squealing with delight.

Rosie unfolds a good linen tablecloth that she begins to spread over the table.

"Mother," Annie complains.

"I'm sorry dear, I want to be ready for the caterer.

Would you put those flowers on the table for me?"

"Here she is," I say, as a new mini-van rolls into the driveway. *City Catering and Banquets* is printed on the door over a stylized piece of pie.

A tall, attractive woman wearing black slacks and a white blouse gets out of the van. A few minutes later she arrives at the door loaded down with packages. Her shoulder-length hair is streaked in a variety of subtle reds, auburns, and blonds. I spring to her aid, taking a number of small containers that are threatening to fall. Her round red lips pronounce the words, thank you. She is probably in her mid-thirties, dresses fashionably, and smells good. Or is it the food?

"This is my daughter, Annie and my husband, Bart," Rosie says.

"How do you do. I'm Enid Pond." She says this with a confident smile. Her hair cuts diagonally across her high cheekbones, her green eyes are very observant. I notice a tiny diamond nestled in the contour of her perfect nose. She goes to work assembling an elegant setting for two with china, polished silverware and linen napkins that go nicely with Rosie's good tablecloth. From a stainless steel container Enid ladles a steaming mushroom concoction into pastry shells with some unpronounceable French name. Rosie and Annie are seated across from one another and both enthuse at the taste and texture of what they call, *the starter*. I can't wait to see *the ender*.

I take our humble soup and sandwiches on a tray up

to the loft where Stu and I chow down. I read the newspaper. *Saska-Boom* announces the headline on the front page of the business section. The article describes how resources, especially oil, potash and uranium and the escalating price of grain are all taking the economy to new heights. It mentions the Okianec Park townhouse development and the recently announced Sombrero plant in Crooked Lake as examples of the growth.

"We chose the mushroom v*ol au vent,*" Annie says later, "and the *crème caramel* for dessert." She watches for my reaction. Rosie looks at me defiantly as each additional course is listed, including generous hunks of organically grown baron of beef. Enid insisted that the only way to do it justice was on a barbecue.

I wonder whatever happened to sausage, perogies and cabbage rolls, the triumvirate that has conveyed countless couples into matrimonial bliss? "How much is all this going to cost?" I ask, with not a little apprehension.

"It won't cost as much as you think and it'll be worth every penny." Rosie makes an unreadable face. "And this caterer will bring something very special to the wedding, I promise you that."

"I'm sure she will, Honey," I say. Thank god Randall's folks are paying for half of this.

Despite the shocking occurrence at the elevator yesterday, the beautiful Indian summer day sees my sometimes-regular foursome out on the golf course. I was hesitant to go, but Rosie encouraged me, saying, "It'll take your mind off things for a while." So I loaded up my clubs and drove the six miles out to the regional park golf course.

Nick Taylor is first off the tee with his usual two hundred and fifty yard drive, followed by Ray Chow, the local doctor, a meticulous player, who lands his ball just a little behind Nick's.

"So, who do you think killed him?" Nick asks, inquisitively.

"I don't know?" I say, warming up with some shoulder rotations.

"What was he like?" Dee Elliot asks.

I lift my eyebrows. "He was a nice guy, but just a regular guy."

"Who ran one of the biggest corporations in the world."

"Yeah, well, all I know is he liked fishing. And besides that, he cared about the environment."

"Yeah, right," Dee scoffs.

"He did."

"What about this terminal they're building?" Nick says. "Did he tell you anything about that?"

"I heard about it same as everybody else," I say.

"Well, it's good news," Nick says, as though there might be a job there for him. Since losing his greens keeper's job at the golf course, Nick has been bouncing from one thing to another. Fortunately his wife, Wilma, has a steady pay cheque coming in.

"Why did you invite Morrison for supper?" Doc Chow says.

That's the same question the cops asked. "Why is it a guy can't invite somebody over for a meal without getting the third degree about it?"

Dee Elliot says, "I guess people are wondering whose side you're on, the local farmers or the corporations."

"What the hell's that supposed to mean?" I say. I know she's only playing devil's advocate, but it galls me to hear that people might be thinking that way.

Dee, who only recently took up golf, slice's one into the thick bush on the right side of the fairway. She's a strong, athletic woman, if a little over weight. Looking at us defiantly through her large red-rimmed glasses, she takes another ball from her bag and hits the exact same shot with the exact same result. No one says a word. Even Nick holds his tongue.

Then Doc says, innocently, "You want to try again?"

Now even Dee doubles over in laughter.

My shot bounces onto the left side of the fairway, safe, but leaving me a long three wood to the green.

"But what did Morrison really come for?" Dee says in a tone reflecting her less than fuzzy feelings for big business.

"To announce the new terminal," I say.

"But they don't need the CEO all the way from Mexico City to announce a project like this plant in Crooked Lake. What are they saying by having him here?"

"What do you think?" Doc says.

"I think it's about staking a claim in Saskatchewan," Dee says. "Knowing that this is their best bet for the future. Knowing there are huge resources here."

"And that bodes well for the economy," Doc says.

"But not for the environment," Dee counters. "And this province ranks only behind Alberta as worst polluter in the country already."

Doc lines up his putt with care, as though intentionally silencing Dee. We all watch, thinking about her words.

"Was it the wheat?" Nick asks, as Doc walks over to retrieve his ball from the cup. "Was he crushed by the wheat?"

The picture had appeared on the front page of every newspaper and on every TV screen. Just one picture had been released by the RCMP. It showed exactly what I saw when I found Lionel. A slender wrist and hand sticking stiffly out of a pile of wheat, frozen fingers pointing to the sky.

But nowhere appeared the polaroid picture that Hutt showed me. In that one Lionel's face was blistered and burned. But worse, his eyeballs were shrivelled up, the sockets almost empty.

"You know I can't talk about my work as coroner," Doc says. "Besides, I don't know what killed him," he adds, almost to himself. I guess even Doc doesn't know what happened to Lionel. "An autopsy will tell the exact cause."

"Any guesses?" Nick asks.

"Look, I just pronounced him deceased." Doc looks at me and swallows hard. "RCMP forensics people took over from there." I remember the rattled look Doc wore emerging from the elevator.

On the third hole with a mighty swing, and despite my allowance for the slice, I send my ball a good twenty yards into a field of standing wheat.

Not to be outdone, Dee tees up and clubs her ball deep into *Suicide Rough,* a wasteland of thistles strewn with rocks and furrows. I notice Doc Chow raise an eyebrow at our antics.

We continue in that vein for the next few holes before arriving at the infamous seventh. The seventh is the hole where a year ago Harvey Kristoff was clubbed to death with Nick Taylor's seven iron. Not the one he's playing with today, of course.

Nick, still with the honours, hits his ball to the right of the green, unfortunately the exact spot where the body was found the previous spring. Nick was exonerated of the crime, but not before being arrested and put through hell as the main suspect in not one, but two murders.

Nick chips his shot on to, and off of the green. The ball rolls down a steep slope and into the brush next to the lake. The lousy shot brings down our collective game even more, evidenced by Doc's bogie on the par three hole.

Mercifully, the game is cut short by a sudden thunderstorm. As the sky opens up, we pile into our carts and trundle off toward the clubhouse. The rain turns to hail that hammers the roofs of the carts.

A number of other golfers are in the clubhouse lounge taking refuge from the storm. They watch the hail accumulate on the deserted first tee. None of it has yet reached golf-ball sized proportions, thankfully.

We order beers all around. Taking a sip of my dark ale, I hear my name being mentioned a few tables over. I try to ignore it, but the speaker gets louder and more strident until I can't ignore it. It's obvious he wants not only me, but all the patrons in the clubhouse to hear him.

When I look over, I recognize Jerry Harper sitting at a table with three other men. It's apparent they arrived long before we did and have built up a good head of steam.

"Fucking Bartowski's making money, anyway," Jerry snarls. "And hey, that's what counts, isn't it?" His dark eyes nail me with a cold stare.

Jerry is lean and hard and good looking, except for a large hooknose. He inherited it from his father's side. Hooknose Harper is what Jerry was called until he was big enough and tough enough and mean enough to kick the shit out of every last person who called him Hooknose. The nose took a beating too, broken several times.

"The bank stole my farm," Jerry says to all who will

listen. "Now they're going to build that goddamned distribution plant on it. And Sombrero got my land at a bargain price too. How about you, Bartowski, did you give them a bargain price at your lodge?"

I try not to react, but everyone in the place has turned to me, waiting for a response. I feel my face flush. "Jerry, I don't know what you're talking about."

"Oh you don't, eh?" he says. "I'm talking about Sombrero coming in here and scooping up my land. And you, hand in glove with them fuckers."

The muscled men at his table, one of whom sports a tattoo on his right forearm, give him grunts of support.

"What's that got to do with me?" I say, sounding braver than I feel.

Jerry took over the family farm when the old man died, and he and his wife Gail raised a few pigs, some chickens, and the rest of the stuff that goes with mixed farming as it used to be called. The era of specialization has become so prevalent we forget about the farmers who used to do it all. Now it's hogs, or cattle, or grain, or what have you.

But since mixed farming doesn't pay that well Jerry and two buddies decided it would be a good idea to go out and steal expensive machinery and turn it over for a quick profit. It wasn't long before they got caught, and Jerry served almost two years at the Regina Correctional Centre, in fact he's still on parole. While he was in jail the bank foreclosed on his farm, and the family has since moved into low-rent housing in town.

Now Jerry drives truck for Agro-Chem, delivering fertilizer and Gail does house cleaning for the home care association.

Doc appeals to Jerry's civility, but Jerry ignores him.

"While I lose my farm, Bartowski gets rich," Jerry says, drunkenly.

I watch Nick lean back in his chair so he can make eye contact with Jerry. "It was your own fault you lost the farm, so shut the fuck up," Nick says.

"Why don't you fuckin' make me?" Jerry raps the tabletop sharply. A couple of longneck bottles fall over. His friends try to calm him down and others echo the sentiment. In response he kicks over his chair. "You'll get yours, Bartowski," he says. "Just like Morrison got his." And with a few more expletives thrown in my direction, he stomps out followed by his buddies. During the short but distinct silence that follows, I realize that the storm has passed.

"He's got a real hard-on for you?" Dee says, as things settle down in the clubhouse lounge.

"Looks like it," I say, shaken by Jerry's hostility towards me.

"The guy's always had a major attitude problem," Nick says. "But you can hardly blame him, growing up with that schnozz, eh?" Nick chuckles.

"Remember when he popped Mr. Lasko, the vice-principal," Dee says. "Jerry figured Lasko had said 'playing hooky' a little too often at a truancy meeting."

"Anyway, I'd watch my back if I were you," Nick says, giving me a grim look. Dee and Doc nod in agreement.

We finish our beers soberly. Other golfers regroup. Some head out and try to continue their interrupted games, but others, like us, are done and take home images of an unpleasant end to a day already spoiled by the hailstorm.

After supper Stuart gazes into the Sears Catalogue. "I like the *Winchester*," he says. "It's a nice size, and the lever action, it's like *The Rifleman*." He lifts his eyebrows animatedly, knowing he'll get a rise out of me. He's been after us for months to let him have a rifle. But having seen Stu grow up on video games using virtual weapons to slaughter infinite numbers of enemies, I'm not anxious to see a real gun in his hands.

"It would take a lot of time to train you," I say. "There'd be weeks of lessons before you'd get live ammo and then, well . . . you've got school."

"You don't have to train me, Dad. The cadet corps is holding a course."

"Oh, they are?" I feel a little left out now.

"After that we have to go out with an experienced hunter," he says, shooting me with his index finger and thumb, "at least three times before we can get a license to hunt on our own."

"What's this about hunting on your own?" Rosie asks, walking in to the kitchen carrying a basket of freshly laundered bed sheets.

"After the course."

"What course?"

Stuart looks over at me as though I'll lend his plan some support. "The Air Cadet Firearm Safety Course," he says, putting a good spin on it.

Rosie's gaze slides my way, and her expression needs no translation.

"Come on, Mom," Stu says, "I'm almost fourteen. Most kids got guns when they were thirteen, even twelve some of them. Besides we got rifles up at the lodge. Don't you think I should know how to use them safely?"

He's got a point there, but still Rosie doesn't concede.

"Here's the one I want," Stu says, pointing to the *Winchester* lever-action .22 calibre rifle in the Sears catalogue. They've even commandeered the image of Chuck Connors, the star of the original *Rifleman* TV series, to flog the thing.

Rosie only glances at it, as though showing any real interest would somehow undermine her opposition to it. "Why don't we sleep on it," she says.

"Okay, we'll talk about it at oh-eight-hundred," Stuart says, resolute. "Besides I'm gonna join the army when I'm eighteen. Then he does a military about face and heads to his room.

Again Rosie's glare accuses me. "Why are you encouraging him?" she says. "Haven't we got enough going on without adding a dangerous weapon into the mix?"

"I have not been encouraging him. But he does have a point about the lodge. Up there it could be a matter of life or death. And if he's going to take over some day."

"And what about this joining the army business?"

"First I've heard of it," I say, "though I'm not surprised, after all he's in cadets, being conditioned for it. Then a recruitment officer shows up with all the bells and whistles. Next thing you know, the kid's signed up."

"That's crazy talk. Stuart's only thirteen." Rosie ignores the fact that he'll only be thirteen for another month.

"He'd have to register a gun," Rosie says.

"I know," I say.

"What about your guns, are they registered?"

"Nope. The program got scrapped."

"After they spent billions on it?"

"Yup."

Rosie shakes her head in disgust.

Rosie and I step out on to the back porch with our morning coffee to watch the sun rise. A swather rolls by in the field behind our house. The big machine mows down wheat with sharpened blades of steel, raking it into swaths to be combined later. Fortunately yesterday's hail was localized and not much crop damage was reported. Harvest will go day and night as long as the weather holds and there's any grain left in the fields.

Our garden too is flush with fall vegetables, including carrots, beets and potatoes. I've already put up the cabbages, though I did lose some of those to the damned worms. But there's enough sauerkraut to last 'till next year. As I head in for more coffee, a flock of snow geese fly overhead calling back and forth in a cacophonous chant. With their sheer numbers they turn fields winter-white this time of year.

"Who is Jerry Harper to criticize us, or anyone else for that matter?" Rosie says, when I tell her about the ugly incident at the golf club. "Why would people listen to him?"

"He has a big beef against the bank and against Sombrero. And he connects us with them."

"He's sure got a wild imagination," Rosie says.

I don't tell her what Jerry said just after he kicked over his chair—*you'll get yours, Bartowski, just like Morrison got his.* What did he mean by that? And is he the one doling out the justice?

Rosie goes inside. A couple of crows perch on the fence, while another checks out the compost heap. Like humans, crows are opportunists and given a chance will move right in. When the banks foreclose, Sombrero swoops in like an enterprising crow discovering unprotected booty.

Inside, Rosie is on the phone. Before hanging up, she says, "Okay, Reverend, I'll tell him."

"Tell me what?"

"The United Church is holding a memorial service for Lionel this morning at eleven o'clock."

"Oh?"

"Reverend Roy said he felt it was our duty since Lionel was killed in Crooked Lake. Apparently Lionel was Lutheran, but Roy figured United was close enough."

There's a good turnout at the service and Rosie and I are forced to squeeze in next to Dee Elliot in the middle of a row. Sitting beside us is an assortment of locals, including Helen Mousie from the Co-op Store and Netty Ostrovsky, the RCMP secretary. In the back pew a familiar looking blonde touches up her makeup while a well-dressed man next to her speaks not so quietly into a cell phone that's hooked to his ear

Sitting in the front pew is Jack Kolchak along with what look like a few other executives from Sombrero. Chas sits across the aisle looking daggers at Kolchak, his muscled head resting on his large fist. I notice Kolchak look back, holding Chas' gaze for a moment.

Reverend Roy has managed to assemble the choir and they hum the *Old Rugged Cross* while a talented kid on the organ applies a gospel feel to the venerable hymn.

"We're here to remember Lionel Jonathan Morrison," Reverend Roy intones, "and to honour this distinguished personage who was so cold-heartedly killed in our community. We are also here to celebrate his life and his ascension to the Promised Land." *We Shall Gather at the River* follows the short sermon.

Then Reverend Roy says, "Anyone who would like to share his or her thoughts on the untimely death of Lionel Morrison is welcome to come up and do so. But first I'd like to invite Mr. Jack Kolchak to say a few words on behalf of Sombrero."

Kolchak steps up to the pulpit. His dark hair is freshly cut and his strong features are strengthened by the light that floods in through the arched windows. "Lionel Morrison was a person who held to his convictions and would not be swayed no matter the opposition." Kolchak's strong voice reverberates through the packed church. "We know that his loss will leave a deep hole in the fabric of our lives and of our company. On behalf of Sombrero Incorporated I want to extend condolences to Lionel's wife, Margaret Morrison, and their daughter, son-in-law and granddaughter, and to the many friends and loved ones who will miss him." Some how I didn't think Kolchak would.

The mayor gets up next. "On behalf of the Town of Crooked Lake I would like to express my sympathy to the family of Lionel Morrison. At the same time we want to assure you that Crooked Lake is a safe town, and this an isolated incident. We also hope that the unfortunate death of Lionel Morrison will not negatively impact the planned Sombrero plant here in Crooked Lake." Apparently nothing's sacred when it comes to local economic development.

A couple of service clubs—Rotary and Lions—bring condolences from their members, then I get up and walk to the front of the church. It's not like I planned it, or even thought about it. My legs just seem to carry me up to the pulpit where I stand feeling completely blank.

Roy gives me an encouraging bob of his head.

"Good morning," I say. "I uh, got up here because I think something needs to be said." I clear my throat. "After spending some time with Lionel Morrison up at my fishing lodge, I found him to be a warm, compassionate human being wanting the same things you and I want."

I look around, now a little embarrassed. Kolchak gives me a shit-eating grin.

"Lionel Morrison cared about the environment," I say. Some groans echo through the church. "Some of you may find that hard to believe. But he was a man who recognized the need for change." I see a familiar face standing at the back of the room, but she's hidden behind a tall, rangy rancher. "I really just wanted to say that Lionel Morrison was not just the CEO of Sombrero. He was an ordinary person like you or me who experienced all the human hurt and happiness there is in life. And for that reason, I'm sorry he's gone."

The old wooden floor squeaks anxiously as I return to my seat and grab Rosie's hand.

Father Lebret from St. Mary's leads the *Lord's Prayer,* including the 'forever and ever' line at the end in deference to the protestant congregation.

The service concludes with Reverend Roy in his lovely tenor voice singing a heartfelt rendition of *Oh, Danny Boy* for the deceased Irishman. Even the blonde reporter's face softens a smidgen, but not enough to ruin her make-up.

Cameras flash and video rolls as the Sombrero party exits the church. A pearl-gray stretch limo stands by.

"Who do you think murdered Lionel Morrison?" a scruffy video reporter shouts, fiercely pointing his camera at Jack Kolchak, who ignores the question.

"Who would gain most by his death?" another reporter asks.

The freshly made-up blonde asks in a friendly voice, "Do you think the CEO of Sombrero was killed because of Sombrero's land grabs?"

Now I recognize her. She's with TOX News. Always

reporting on the sensational stuff.

As other questions fly from the scrum, Kolchak gets up onto the church step, putting him a head above everyone else. Microphones and cameras home in on him. He pushes his thick hair back with both hands and buttons his suit jacket.

"I want to respond to that question," he says in his precise baritone. "Firstly, I would like to say that you—Kolchak's dark eyes spike the blonde reporter, who tries to look cool and unperturbed—have asked a very rude question, given we're at a man's memorial." The two stare each other down like a dog and cat. "However, I will say this," he goes on, "Sombrero will not change its acquisition policies because of the death of its CEO. And in response to the Mayor's concerns regarding our Crooked Lake distribution terminal, Lionel Morrison's death will not affect our plans here in any way."

Cameras click and whir and whiz. "Do you think the RCMP will find the murderer?" the reporter with the cell phone attached to his ear asks.

"I have every confidence in the RCMP. In fact, I have been asked by my company to liaise with the police in the investigation of our CEO's death," Kolchak says.

"Do the police have any suspects?" the scruffy video reporter shouts.

"Why don't you ask them?" Kolchak points to the long, low station wagon that's parked across the street.

The passenger side window emits a cloud of illicit smoke.

"Or ask Mr. Bartowski," Kolchak says when he notices me, "he's the one that found the body."

A frenzy of reporters turns on Rosie and me. Even Dee Elliot joins them.

Questions are thrown at me willy-nilly. Rosie and I try to walk away but get cornered between the concrete church steps and a thick lilac hedge. Rosie stands stolidly next to me, grasping my arm.

A CBC reporter that I recognize jumps in. "This is not the first dead body you've found, is it?"

The throng bristles at the news. I feel like a deer in the headlights as the gang presses closer.

"What other bodies have you found? What were you doing at the elevator? Who do you think killed Morrison?"

"Tell us about the hand," the scruffy video-reporter shouts."

Rosie elbows me in the ribs and whispers, "Say something, or we'll never get out of here."

"I'm sorry, but I've been instructed by the police not to say anything." I nod toward the detectives who now stand leaning against their unmarked unit.

The reporters turn and look at Hutt and Klassen and as they do, Rosie and I make our escape, hurrying along the leafy lilac hedge to my pickup truck.

We get in and I'm about to pull away from the curb when we're blocked by the bulk of Sergeant Hutt with Detective Klassen standing at attention next to him.

Hutt comes around to my window. "Hello, Bart." A

few wisps of hair fly freely in the breeze from his balding head. He tries to palm them under control, without much success. "I'd like to talk to you," he says.

Klassen has closed in on the other side of the truck. Rosie rolls up her window.

"We were just about to go for dinner," I say, imploringly. My stomach had repeatedly reminded me and some of my neighbours during the service that it was time to eat.

Hutt doesn't look happy, but maybe in deference to Rosie, he says, "Come down to the station after that."

"Will do," I say.

The camera crews are now setting up to film their reports. Some have chosen Crooked Lake's elevators as backdrop to their stories, others the quaint, white clapboard church.

Soon we're sitting in a window booth at the Junction Stop Café. Farm caps mix with the coiffed hair of travellers on their way to or from Saskatoon, fifty miles to the southwest. The Junction Stop is kept busy serving meals and gas to motorists who converge at highways 4 and 37. We watch, as many of the media people arrive at the already crowded restaurant.

Rosie orders a hot chicken sandwich while I opt for the pork chops. The waitress, a heavy, bespectacled woman, takes our orders and fills our cups with steaming hot coffee.

"Busy around here," I observe.

She sticks her pencil into a nest of hair just above her left ear, then wipes perspiration off her forehead with the back of her hand. "It's been like this ever since . . . well, you know, since that Morrison fella died. All kinds of strangers in town." She picks up the coffee thermos off the table. "City folk, eh? I'll tell you one thing, we don't see tips like this very often. They leave fifteen percent on top of their bill, sometimes even more. We're lucky if these locals leave us anything." Then she smiles uneasily. "Not all locals, of course."

The CBC reporter and his camera operator stroll by and take a recently vacated table in the corner. Others, including the blonde from TOX, are not so lucky.

"Those reporters are something, aren't they?" Rosie says. "Especially that one." She nods toward the TOX reporter who stands near the entrance casting about for an open seat.

Without the microphone in her hand she looks a little less daunting, though no less glamorous, in that *blonde* way.

"She's not afraid to ask the hard questions, eh?" Rosie says.

"I guess that's what she gets paid the big bucks for," I say. "And this *is* one hell of a big story."

Rosie raises her eyebrows at that and watches more reporters and camera crews arrive. There appears to be no love lost between the TOX reporter and the others. The TOX News crew is buffed and tattooed as though meant to physically dominate scrums.

As I cut happily into my chop, the waitress returns with her coffee pot. But this time in addition to topping up our cups, she slides a piece of folded paper onto the table and nods in the TOX reporter's direction.

I'd like an interview, the note says. *Will pay, handsome. Let's talk, Tara Spencer.*

"It's from her," I say, nodding toward Tara Spencer who's found a seat at the counter.

"What does it say?" Rosie asks.

"She wants an interview." Did she make a mistake, or did I read it wrong. *Handsome?*

When I look over at Tara Spencer, she rotates on her stool and raises her cup. A short red skirt showcases long, shapely legs. And I'm pretty sure I didn't read the note wrong.

"She's cute," Rosie says in a way I've come to dread.

"She says she'll pay," I say, trying to slide by how cute Ms Spencer is and slipping the note into my back pocket at the same time.

"Isn't that unethical?" Rosie says.

"What?"

"Paying for news interviews."

I paste my lips together and look ignorant. "I'm not sure."

"Are you going to talk to her?"

"What have I got to lose?" I say.

"What indeed?" Rosie gives me a look as if to say she doesn't miss a trick. She slides out of the booth. I pay for the meal and leave an exorbitant tip of two dollars and twenty-five cents. Fifteen percent, exactly.

I drop Rosie off at Hazel's Hair Hut where she's having her hair styled for the wedding. She's been talking about it for weeks, even asking my opinion, which I refrain from offering.

At the police station Sergeant Hutt greets me and tries to make small talk, but it's obvious his heart's not in it. Klassen assumes his usual pseudo-military stance, this time the ill-at-ease position.

"When Morrison was up at your lodge," Hutt says, "did he give you any idea who might want to see him dead?"

"Of course not." I'm disturbed by the question. "I was not party to any confidences of Lionel Morrison. All we ever talked about was fishing."

"And you never met him before?"

"No."

"What about the other Sombrero people?"

"No. First time anybody from their company has been at the lodge." These are questions that I've answered before. I'm wondering when they're going to get to the point.

Hutt moves uncomfortably on his chair. "This Chas, the assistant-slash-bodyguard, from who was he protecting Morrison?"

"Why don't you ask him?"

"Don't you worry about him," Klassen says, "let's just stick with your story."

We pause for a moment as the office comes alive, dispatching a constable to the scene of an accident on Main Street.

"What about Kolchak? What do you know about him?"

"Not much, except he seems to be the ambitious type. But I guess that's what it takes to succeed in the corporate world."

"And Chas? Could he have stayed at the motel because he knew the thing was going down?" I think they just got to the point.

"I don't know, but I doubt it. He seemed devoted to Lionel. Very loyal."

"And a loyal Yankees fan too," Klassen sneers.

The two detectives grill me until we've gone over all of the details from when I met Morrison on the floatplane dock to when I read the time on the watch that graced his frail wrist as it emerged from that pile of wheat.

Hutt gets to his feet. He's been twitching and is probably craving a smoke. On my way out I hear the accident on Main Street was a collision between a bicycle and a pedestrian. The senior who was struck by the bicycle complained that she had every right to walk across the street to get from the post office to the Lucky Dollar Bakery. And furthermore, there should be a cross walk to that effect. No one was seriously injured, and no charges were laid.

I swing by the Co-op store to pick up the things on

Rosie's list. It's mostly non-perishables for our final week at the lodge when we will host some regulars from Dallas, Texas.

"There he is," Helen says, "our local celeb."

"Give me a break, eh?" I say.

Helen chuckles and begins ringing in my items. "Quite a little speech you made at the memorial," she says. Her plump head leans coyly to one side.

"Yeah?"

"You sounded like a real Sombrero booster."

"What?"

"That's what some people said." Her jowls jiggle.

"I never even mentioned Sombrero."

She looks at me, her large eyes unmoving. "By the way, I had René in here yesterday." She begins bagging my groceries.

"Yeah?" I say.

"Had the usual complaints. He didn't look too good."

"Thanks," I say, taking my bags, "I'll drop in on him."

When Rosie comes out of Hazel's she walks self-consciously down the sidewalk and gets into the truck.

Her long blonde tresses have been shorn and what's left is a frenzy of tousled curls that hang loosely about her face. I say my rehearsed line, the one I use whenever I'm asked for an opinion on Rosie's appearance. "Looks good."

"Hazel's good," Rosie deflects the compliment.

I'm a little shocked she's cut it so short. "Short," I

say, before I can stop myself.

She gives me a sidelong glance. "You hate it."

"No, not at all. It's a definite improvement," I say.

"What do you mean by that?" She says.

"Nothing," I say, "it's perfect." Then I shut my mouth.

At home Annie praises the hairdo, though she shares a raised eyebrow with me.

But soon the new do is forgotten and Rosie and Annie are engrossed in wedding plans. Annie proposes a change to the menu.

"What now?" Rosie says.

"And how much?" I put in.

"It's nothing Daddy. I just want to change the dessert."

"Well, what is the dessert?" I ask.

"That's not the point," Rosie says. "We've got to finalize the menu."

"*Crème Caramel,*" Annie says with a French accent. Enid Pond did one hell of a sales job on these two.

"I want something more local, you know, like Saskatoon berry pie."

"Well," I say, relieved, "that sounds good to me."

"It'll cost an extra hundred bucks," Rosie says.

"What?" But just as I'm about to object more vociferously, the phone rings.

"Mr. Bartowski," a well-modulated voice says. "This is Tara Spencer, TOX News."

"Let me take this in my office," I say. Rosie and Annie look relieved, as I make my way down to the bear pit.

"What can I do for you?" I say, picking up the office phone.

"As I said in my note, I'd like an interview, and I can make it worth your while."

"I don't really have a lot to say," I reply.

"You let me worry about that."

"Is it usual practice to pay for interviews?" I ask, not feeling much enthusiasm for the whole idea.

"In certain instances we like to offer an incentive," she says.

"And in this instance?"

"We feel it's in the public interest. It also allows us to edit the footage according to our needs."

"Which means what exactly?"

"We can discuss that when we meet," she says. "I'll get back to you."

"I don't know," I say. But it's hard to refuse a beautiful woman, especially when she's offering cash.

By the time I climb the stairs, the dessert has been changed, and an additional two hundred dollars is added to the catering bill—what's pie without ice cream—now it's up to twenty bucks a head. I should probably let Randall's folks know what the total is looking like so they won't bust a gut when I present them with the final tally.

––––––––––

My old friend and former neighbour, René Robert, who just turned ninety, now lives at Lakeview Lodge, a cluster of single-story brick buildings for seniors. Though René suffers from arthritis, loss of hearing, and is partially blind, his brain works just fine and his memory is like a steel trap.

"Morning René," I say, stepping into his windowed room. He wears a white shirt and his pants are pulled up almost to his armpits and held there by a colourful pair of suspenders that match his rheumy blue eyes.

"What's good about it?" he rejoins in his cantankerous voice, peering about my person for the bottle I sometimes bring him.

"Well, the sun is shining," I say, "and we're still above ground."

"That's not necessarily a good thing," he growls as he cradles his wrist in his palm and grimaces. He wears copper bracelets, but despite that and a daily dose of nettle tea, he still suffers the pain of arthritis. "I could sure use some relief from this goddamned thing," he says.

I pull a slim bottle of rye out of my jacket pocket. "Maybe this will help," I say.

"There's glasses over there," he says, a little more

brightly, pointing to the top of his dresser, over which hangs his picture of Mt. Everest. He says it's a reminder that the whole world isn't flat. I pour us each a short shot.

Examining his glass, he says, "What do you call that?" I add a couple more fingers of rye and hand it over. He drinks most of it in one gulp and expels the fumes with a satisfied wheeze. "Damn, that's good. Around here they won't let me have a drink. Say it's no good for me. Christ I'm ninety years old. I should know what's good for me, don't you think?" He takes another healthy swallow and with a crooked grin says, "How're those brats of yours?" He pauses to turn up his hearing aid. "When are you going to bring 'em around?"

"Annie's wedding preparations are in high gear," I say. "She's looking forward to seeing you there."

I brought René's invitation on my previous visit, but he pooh-poohed the idea of attending, saying, "What's an old fart like me going to do at a wedding?"

"I know Annie would consider it an honour if you came," I say.

René bares his strong, even teeth. "Not a cash bar, is it?"

"No, no," I say. I'd suggested it, but it was shot down by every one. "In fact my job is to pick up the liquor," I say. My one and only chore to date. This wedding may be working out better than I thought.

"Well, maybe," René says, giving his head a shake. "And Stu?"

"He wants a rifle," I say.

"That blessed kid," René says, affectionately. "So what are you going to get him?"

"Well, we haven't quite decided on that yet."

"You get him a good one," René says, gruffly, "maybe a *Winchester.*"

"You think?"

"Well, it's what *The Rifleman* used."

I smell something fishy. "Have you been talking to Stuart?"

"What about this Morrison thing?" René says, ignoring my question. He uses a clean white handkerchief to wipe a little watery discharge that spills down his cheek. "And you're right in the middle of it aren't you?"

"I certainly didn't ask to be," I say.

René clears his throat loudly and holds out his empty glass with a fairly steady hand. "So, tell me about it."

Back at home I'm watching over Emma while Annie goes for her walk. I gaze at my granddaughter as she sleeps. Arguably the most beautiful sight in the world. As I adore her she smiles beatifically and takes a deep satisfying breath. Then slowly she begins to wriggle. Her little fists ball up and make like she wants to box. Then her pudgy legs start kicking, her mouth twists into a frown and her brow furrows. Finally her eyes pop open, revealing a look of sheer terror mixed with rage, all precipitating a furious, "Whaaaaaaaaaaaaa."

Then, just as she crescendos and is taking a frighteningly long breath in preparation for the second act, I hear Annie's voice in the kitchen. Thank god.

After Emma is fed, Rosie and I and Annie and Stuart sit down to dinner.

"I just spoke to Randy, and he's got job offers with two different companies," Annie announces as we dig into the hot *chilli.*

"Where?" Rosie says, always afraid of change.

"Pass the bread," Stuart says. He slathers the slice with butter.

"He's got one," Annie can hardly sit still, "in Vancouver."

"It's so far," Rosie says.

"Mom, it's a lot closer than Iqualuit. And it's Vancouver for gosh sakes."

"What's so great about Vancouver?" Rosie says, looking worried.

"Come on, Mom. The weather, the ocean, the mountains, the shopping, you name it."

She has a few good points, I must admit, especially after the brutal winters we've been having lately.

"Can I come and visit?" Stuart says. His hockey hero plays for the Canucks.

"Where's the other job?" Rosie says.

"Newfoundland."

"Oh, Lord." Rosie stops breathing. I put my hand over hers.

"Can I come see you there?" Stuart asks, still

lobbying for a visit.

After dinner Dee Elliot is hunched over her keyboard, and hardly looks up when I enter *the Reporter*. Her eyes follow scribbled notes as her fingers fly over the keys. Out on Main Street a pick-up truck goes by. Dee keeps tapping away. Another pick-up goes by. After several minutes, she stops.

"I just had to get this finished," she says, as the printer comes to life. "It's for this week's edition."

"What's the story about?" I ask.

"Organic farming," Dee says. "I pulled it all together so it'll make sense to local farmers."

"You don't expect the farmers around here to start organic farming, do you?" I say.

Dee shrugs as she reaches for her Roughriders travel mug. "They're doing it everywhere else, "she says.

"Yeah, but around here the farmers are using all the chemicals they can lay their hands on to get a decent crop off."

"It's because of those chemicals that the soil is so depleted," Dee says. "The stuff strips the land of its natural ability to hold moisture, to fight disease, to combat pests."

"From what I hear it takes a long time to convert to organic farming," I say. "What do farmers do in the mean time?"

"A farmer might be better off to leave his fields fallow for a couple of years, give them a rest, that'll put him half way there."

"Half way?"

"It takes four years to certify."

"Who can live on nothing for four years? At least when a farmer puts a crop in, he gets crop insurance."

"They can still put crops in, but can't use chemicals for four years. They often plow the crops under to replenish the soil. There are some grants available through the department of agriculture."

The printer stops and Dee straightens the sheaf of papers on the counter top. Dee returned to Crooked Lake after living on the west coast for over twenty years. She came back and took over the paper when her dad died. Now she lives in his old house on the outskirts of town where she keeps her sway-backed mare and a few chickens.

Our discussion comes to an abrupt end when a woman walks in and Dee puts on her other cap, that of Sears catalogue agent. The woman sets a tiny dog on the counter and in baby talk says to it, "Such a good Muffy." Muffy yaps at us a few times before exploring the desk top.

Riffling through a stack of papers attached to a clipboard, Dee tells the woman that her order has not arrived. "Should be in tomorrow," Dee says.

The woman looks over and blushes when she sees me sitting there. "Long time no see, Doris." I say.

No one sees much of Doris. She usually hangs around home with her long-time boyfriend Les Thatcher from the post office. When she does go out she's never without her Chihuahua. Even takes him to the movies Saturday nights. Romantic, eh?

"Waiting for something special?" I say.

"Oh . . ." She looks a little embarrassed.

"I'm sorry, I didn't mean to pry."

"No, that's okay," she says. "I ordered a rifle. For Les. Duck hunting, you know." She smiles and reaches for Muffy who's taken up with the tape dispenser.

"What kind of gun did she order?" I ask after they leave.

"Twenty gauge shotgun."

"Pretty hard to shoot ducks with that," I say.

"Good for close range."

"A woman can handle it too," I say.

"Maybe for protection?"

"It's kind of extreme to be buying a gun for protection in Crooked Lake, isn't it?" I say.

"You know Les, paranoid and bag-of-hammers bright." Though I think Doris and little Muffy rule the roost in that house.

"I want to order a gun too," I say.

"Sure you do." Dee laughs.

"I do," I say, raising my eyebrows, seriously.

"You think you need something for protection too?"

"Yeah, from guys like Les."

Dee chuckles again.

"It's actually for Stu." I pull out the page from the Sears catalogue that Stu insisted I bring along and set it on the counter. "This is the one he wants." I point to the *Winchester* lever action twenty-two that's circled in black marker. "And he wants this strap."

Dee looks at me sceptically, but starts tapping the information into her computer.

At breakfast this morning Stu was very convincing on the rifle issue. Rosie was equally persuasive. I sat on the proverbial fence, not wanting to get on anybody's bad side. Rosie finally relented, putting me in charge of the whole thing. Sometimes it doesn't pay to sit on the fence.

———————

I'm reading the newspaper and enjoying my morning coffee when the phone rings. The melodic African voice of Dr. Roger Tweenes is low on the other end of the line. I have to ask him to speak up. Roger is a visiting doctor from the Ivory Coast where he worked mainly with HIV-AIDS afflicted patients. He is here training with our local doctor, Ray Chow.

"I've got the results for your medical," he says.

"Yes?" I say.

"Everything looks normal. Except one of the tests came back positive."

"Oh? Which one?" I ask.

"Your PSA." His tone suggests it's not a good one to come back positive.

"What's that?" I say.

"It has to do with the prostate gland."

"I've heard of it."

"It means that your blood contains indicators . . ."

"Yes?"

"There are some . . ."

"Don't soft-pedal it, Roger."

"It's not conclusive by any means," he says, "but there are moderately high PSA levels pointing to the possibility of prostate cancer." Even his dulcet tones cannot soften the hammering blow of the words.

"Oh." Neither of us speaks for a few moments. The phone rings somewhere in the clinic. I wonder what problem the caller will have. Will it be prostate cancer, like me? Ain't that a zinger? I'm having a hard time catching my breath. It's like my body wants to give up already.

"You must remember," Roger says, as if reading my mind, "good health starts with a positive attitude." His gentle voice is filled with compassion.

"What causes prostate cancer?" I say, grasping how little I know about it.

"The cause is unknown, like most cancers, but the risk factors include advancing age, heredity, hormonal influences, and possibly environmental factors like toxins, industrial products and chemicals.

"Like farm chemicals?"

"Yes."

"Have I been poisoned by them? I've lived next to farmland my whole life."

"We can't say with any certainty I'm afraid," Roger says.

Yeah. I'm afraid too.

The handset is still warm from my harrowing conversation with the doctor when Larry Ludgate, my accountant, calls. He's on the phone from Winnipeg and his voice seems awful quiet too. I ask him twice to speak up. Finally I hear him say, "Didn't you get the notice?"

"What notice?" I say.

"From the CRA."

"About what?"

"The audit."

"Audit?" I'd left the mail unopened in the office the last few days. I feel a chill run up and down my spine. "Are you serious?"

"Dead serious," Larry says, tonelessly.

"I really don't need this right now, Larry," I say, trying not to cry.

"When would you need it?" Larry says, dryly.

"Why me?"

"Luck of the draw," Larry says, "or maybe they got wind from Regina that you're closing up shop."

"I'm not closing up shop," I say, in exasperation.

"I know that," Larry says, "but when they didn't renew your lease last year, the system may have assumed you were going out of business."

"And now the vultures come in to get their piece, right? Why don't they go after some of those crooked corporations before they come after my measly few dollars."

"We've kept your taxes down," Larry says, "but we've played it pretty conservatively."

Larry has been my accountant for years, but I must say I've never heard him use the word *play* in regard to my taxes before. Even though he lives in Winnipeg, Larry, who grew up in Crooked Lake, still does my accounting and tax work. Now he visits once a year. We look at the books, and when that's done, we drink and bullshit until we run out of both, and then he goes home.

"We'll have no problem as long as you just answer their questions," Larry says. "Don't volunteer any information, especially if it's something you haven't told me about. In a case like that, I would have to plead ignorance and you'd be on your own." He clears his throat.

I'm not sure what he's getting at. But he says nothing more, just clears his throat again.

"So what's the next step?" I say, with growing anguish.

"They'll want to check things out for themselves."

"Like what?"

"They look for signs of wealth beyond your means. New home, recent renovations, vehicles, boats. And they check your bank accounts, investments, even your safety deposit box . . ."

"No way," I say.

"It's called full disclosure," he says.

"Am I going to have to pull down my pants too?"

"That's the spirit," Larry says, before hanging up.

The next caller is not quiet, nor do I have to ask her to speak up. "Mr. Bartowski, this is Tara Spencer, are you ready to give me that interview?"

"I suppose," I say. Maybe it'll take my mind off all the good news I've been getting.

"Could we do it at your house?" she says.

I can't think of an excuse, so I say, "I guess so."

"Twenty minutes?" she says.

"Fine."

"Who was that?" Rosie says, pulling on her coat.

"The reporter from TOX. Wants to do that interview."

"And?"

"She's coming over."

"Thanks for the warning."

"You're on your way out, anyway," I say.

"That suits you, doesn't it?"

"What do you mean by that?"

"I saw how you looked at that woman."

I shake my head. "You can stick around."

"We need some things for supper," she says, buttoning her coat. She grabs her shopping bags on the way out.

I tidy up the living room, putting newspapers, magazines, and Rosie's thick paperback on the bottom rack of the coffee table. When the doorbell rings, I take a look in the hall mirror. My gut is gently straining at my belt, my hair is in need of a cut, and I'm dressed in a less than stylish flannel shirt and jeans. Oh, well, what's a poor country boy to do?

"Hello," Tara Spencer says. Up close she's not quite as impressive as from a distance. Her eyes look a little tired and the makeup is layered on pretty thick.

"Come in," I say.

And with that, the buffed TOX crew pushes past me,

carrying armloads of camera gear and sausage-size cables. They begin moving furniture around, one of them searches for outlets and asks where the breaker box is. They set up lights and a camera on a wheeled tripod. Tara is gazing into a compact mirror applying wide swaths of ruby-red lipstick to her slightly thin lips. She adjusts her sweater, so her generous cleavage is shown to best advantage, as the cameraman counts down, silently ending with two, then one finger.

Tara turns to the camera. "We're here today with Bart Bartowski, the Crooked Lake man who discovered the body of Lionel Morrison, the CEO of Sombrero Incorporated, who died in this small Saskatchewan town four days ago."

Tara turns to me and I feel my face flush. "You met Lionel Morrison before he died, did you not?"

"Yes," I say, haltingly.

"Could you tell our audience the circumstances of that meeting?"

"Well," I say, "Mr. Morrison was part of a group of fishermen that spent a week up north at my fishing lodge."

"And the name of the lodge?"

"Stuart Lake Lodge," I say, looking into the camera for the first time.

"When was that?"

"Last week. They flew up on Monday then returned to Saskatoon on Friday afternoon."

"We understand that Lionel Morrison was announcing a

major project that Sombrero is undertaking here in Crooked Lake." She gives me an encouraging nod.

"He announced that they are planning to build a new distribution terminal just north of town. It would service the whole northeast part of the province."

"We heard rumours that some people are not happy with the project."

"I don't know. There are those who believe," I say, thinking of what Dee Elliot said, "that multinationals are buying up all the land and taking over."

"Which would not make the farmers too happy?" Tara says.

"I suppose not," I say, non-commitally.

"Which brings me to my next question. Do you think a farmer had something to do with Morrison's death?"

"I couldn't say one way or the other."

"In other words there is a fifty-fifty chance it was a farmer?"

"I didn't say there's a fifty-fifty chance it was a farmer."

"I just have a few more questions before we go?" Tara says, sweetly.

I can feel the hook sinking into my cheek. "Like what?" I say.

"The hand sticking out of the wheat," she says.

"Yeah?"

"Did you know who it belonged to before they identified the body?"

"No," I say. I did recognize Lionel's multi-dialled watch, but I'm not going to tell her.

"So, you were surprised when the victim turned out to be Lionel Morrison?"

Before I can answer, the door opens with a clatter as Stu arrives home. "Hey, what's going on, Dad? What's TOX doing here?" Stu is in full cadet uniform, having been at his Saturday drill practice.

"They're just leaving," I say.

"You guys are from TOX, eh?" Stu says. "Cool."

Everybody gives Stu a big smile and a high five.

Tara reaches over and shakes his hand. "I'm . . ."

"I know," Stu says, "Tara Spencer. You guys rock."

"Okay, okay, enough," I say.

Stu gravitates over to the camera and Tara says, "Off the record, is there a farmer that you think might have killed Morrison?"

"I didn't say a farmer killed Morrison," I say, though Jerry Harper's words at the golf course do come to mind. "But that's police business. So if you and your crew could . . ." I stretch my arm out toward the door.

"Okay. No hard feelings?" She holds out her hand.

As she leans forward she trips on a cable and uses my shoulder for support. "I'm sorry," she says, laughing. With my arm around her, her cleavage becomes my focal point for a split second.

It's during that split second that I hear Rosie say, "What's going on here, Bart?" She stands at the entrance to the dining room, a bag of groceries in each hand.

"Nothing, Honey," I say, pulling my eyes away from Tara's bosom and pointing to the door. "These people were just leaving."

Stu is now behind the camera training it on Rosie.

"I was in the process of ushering them out when you arrived," I say.

"Yeah, it sure looked like it."

"What do you mean by that? Stuart, quit that," I say, waving away the camera he's now pointing at me.

"And what's happened to my furniture?" Rosie says. The dining room has been stripped of its table and chairs and contains only two tall stools and spindly-legged light stands. Rosie deposits the grocery bags onto the kitchen counter, turns and stalks out of the room. The camera follows.

Having cleared the TOX crew out, put away the groceries and started supper, I feel well on my way to redeeming myself. After all, I was not pawing Tara, she'd just lost her balance on one of those sausage-size cables that were snaking around the floor.

I turn on all-talk radio to find out what's happening in the world. The main item is still Lionel's murder. There's been nothing more shocking to displace it yet. But the police have little to report. After the news, Rosie comes out and eyes me coldly.

"It's about time somebody came up with an idea to help women in the kitchen," I say, closing the freezer drawer of our new bottom-mount refrigerator. "Imagine how many sore backs a fridge like this will save among the housewives of the world." I open the fridge door and retrieve veggies from the crisper.

"Why are you talking like such a sexist?" Rosie says.

"Because I know it bugs you," I say, wiping my hands on my apron.

"And you want to bug me?"

"Yes," I prod her shoulder.

"And why's that?" She pushes back.

"Because I like to bug you."

"You know what bugs me," she says. "Every time a good looking woman's around you jump up and down like a poodle with a stiffy."

"What? That's not true."

"It sure is. And don't think I don't notice. "

"Come on . . ."

"Even with that Enid Pond. All of a sudden he's Mr. Charming himself. All helpful and enthusiastic."

"Why is it that you're so insecure about other women?" I say.

Rosie makes no response.

Oh-oh. Was that below the belt? "Because you're always the most beautiful woman in the room," I say, hoping to save myself.

"Yeah, right," she says.

"Are you kidding, you've got the face of an angel and the body of a . . ."

But she isn't listening. She's riveted to something she hears on the radio. All of a sudden her eyes widen and her mouth opens. She runs to turn up the volume.

In his exclusive interview with TOX News, Bartowski who discovered Sombrero CEO Lionel Morrison's body suggested that it might be a farmer who is responsible for Morrison's death. In an interview released this afternoon, Bartowski says he thinks there is a fifty-fifty chance that a farmer committed the murder.

"You didn't say that?" Rosie says, unbelieving.

"Well, no . . ." The phone rings and I go over to pick it up.

"Are you seeing this?" It's Dee Elliot.

"No, but I'm getting an earful on the radio."

"What were you thinking?"

"I wasn't," I say.

"They've even got you and Rosie in a bit of a row. Not to mention you sneaking a peak at Tara's boobs, which I admit are pretty nice, but still."

"Jesus," I say. "I guess I better go see what's going on." I hang up the phone. I put my arm around Rosie's shoulder, but she shrugs it off. We go down to the rec room in the basement and switch on the TV.

Tara Spencer's face fills the screen, I turn up the volume.

When I wake up Sunday morning, it's one of those blustery, cloudy days when you could just as easily go right back to bed. But everything's changed since yesterday's TOX report and there's no going back. Not only have I been inundated by calls from the media, but I've had to endure countless condemnations from irate farmers suggesting that I do anatomically impossible things to myself. I tried to call Tara Spencer and the producers of her show, anybody from TOX. Nobody would answer, recorded messages sent me around in circles.

After toast and coffee, I dress for church. Soon I'm pacing back and forth in the kitchen waiting for Rosie who is helping Annie with the baby. Stu is still in bed. After two years of struggling to get him to church, we finally gave up. I guess he'll go to hell. Mind you, the Pope now says there is no hell, so maybe there's nothing to worry about after all. But I think I'll hedge my bets, and an hour a week in a pew is little enough attention paid to my soul. And the nine AM service leaves us plenty of day left to do with what we want.

At five minutes to nine, Annie emerges carrying Emma who smiles delightedly, waving both arms and legs. Rosie brings up the rear and we're off.

The congregation is made up mostly of old timers, but a few young families have begun to attend as well. We've even got a few kids in Sunday school again.

Reverend Roy's sermon this week, rather than providing answers to my various dilemmas, dwells on the malevolent nature of methamphetamines, better known as crystal meth.

"We've lost more than one of our native sons to the clutches of this heinous crystal. Those who traffic in these life and death drugs," Roy raises his hands, "must be thrown from the chapel." His voice projects from speakers set strategically throughout the church for the largely hearing-impaired congregation. "Though crystal meth is of great concern because of its highly addictive nature," Roy goes on, "in our community we deal more widely with another menace, marijuana. And while crystal meth requires an abomination of chemicals to produce, marijuana is like a gift of nature.

But, sadly, it is no longer nature's gift, but rather a curse on society wrought by organized crime and the government's equally nefarious war on drugs. And not only does today's weed breed crime, but it's ten times stronger than it was when I . . . that is, uh, back in the day. And that means our young people are stoned out of their minds on this stuff. All they can do is sit around and eat. Now, is that what you want for your children? And we've seen child obesity grow enormously. I know if I had any children," and Lord knows, despite being tall and gangly, slightly balding and pushing sixty, the Reverend is still actively seeking a wife, "I would be very careful. Drugs can be extremely seductive, especially for those who have yet to find the Lord. So, I hope you'll all think about what I've said today," the Reverend continues. "Should anyone want further guidance on these or any other personal issues, please see me. May God bless these words to thy holy Name. Next week's sermon will be on the evils of alcohol." A number of parishioners who were nodding in agreement with the reverend's earlier comments now avert their eyes. "Let us bow our heads in prayer."

Prayer? Even with my mortality staring me in the face I wonder if there is a God to pray to, and if there is, if He/She/It will answer my prayer. I look over at Rosie. Her eyes are closed, but a tear escapes her lowered lid. I put my arm around her and hold her close.

After church we drive the four blocks home and change into civvies.

"I noticed a couple of your friends in church today," I say to Stu who's hunched over a bowl of corn flakes, still wearing his pajamas.

"Yeah, who were they?"

When I tell him he makes a face.

"What's wrong with them?" I ask.

"Nothing," Stu says, like I wouldn't understand.

"You know, Stu," Rosie says, "you missed a wonderful sermon today."

"Yeah, like Moses parted the sea," Stu says, "or Josh

fit the battle of Jericho?"

"No," Rosie says, "it was about crystal meth and marijuana."

"Reverend Roy smokes himself," Stu says, almost choking on his cereal.

"He does not," Rosie says, indignantly.

Annie nods her head at me.

"The point is," Rosie says, "that marijuana is sold by organized criminals. And it's very, very strong. And all you want to do is eat, apparently," she adds, with a puzzled look.

Annie and Stu laugh. I'm not sure what to think, so I head for the refrigerator. Though our new fridge is half again as large as the old one it still manages to get filled to capacity and then some.

"How about an omelette?" I say, pulling out eggs, cheese and green pepper.

Everyone's hungry and over our omelettes we continue a lively discussion about the drug problem. The kid's solution is always to legalize it.

Though it's still blustery out it doesn't look like rain, so I slip out to the driving range for some much needed practice. With a bucket of balls in hand I find a t-box at the end of the line. There's an athletic looking woman hitting balls at the other end. Her movements are natural, her swing powerful. Looking a little closer, I realize it's Enid Pond. I wonder what she's doing in town? Today she wears shorts, exposing athletic, but still curvaceous legs. With what seem like effortless strokes, she knocks balls two hundred plus yards. I pull my hat down in an attempt to remain anonymous.

There are a couple of kids whacking balls with no particular interest in seeing where they go. A nervous mother watches her husband show their five-year-old how to use his pint-sized driver.

It feels good swinging a club. My first drive goes long and straight. I try to replicate the shot, with some success. The third shot has a minor slice. The fourth, a major slice. On the fifth, I change clubs. My trusty nine iron always brings back my natural swing. But even it betrays me.

It's just then Enid sings out, "Hello."

I try to pretend I don't hear.

Then, "Hello, Bart."

I turn and do my surprised act.

"How are you doing?" she says, examining me head to toe.

"Oh, just fine, I say, except for this." I hold up my club and try to laugh it off.

"I can help you with that slice."

Great, she was watching the whole thing.

"Would you like a few pointers?" she says, nodding toward her t-box.

"I guess," I say, feeling embarrassed and, I'll admit, a little emasculated.

Clutching my wretched driver and equally wretched nine iron, I follow her over to her tee-box. My eyes seem to have a mind of their own as she walks ahead of me, her long tanned legs carrying her well-toned body. When she turns, her turquoise eyes are shaded by generous lashes and separated by that perfect diamond-studded nose.

As luck would have it, her lesson necessitates grasping her from behind and gripping her wrists to get the feel of the swing that will straighten out my slice. We grind together from back swing to follow through.

"And again," she says. "And again. And again. Now, on your own." She moves, so she can face me.

I try to hide my enthusiasm behind the narrow shaft of my driver. I tee up my ball, take a practice swing, and then hit the worst slice of my life.

"Well, that didn't help." Enid laughs.

"I was distracted," I say.

"By what?" she asks, innocently.

"Okay. So I'm a terrible golfer."

She laughs again. "You are not."

"You're quite a golfer," I say. "Where did you learn?"

She looks off toward the lake. "My dad was a great golfer. I played with him, up until he died."

"Oh," I say. "I'm sorry."

"It's okay." Enid hesitates a moment, as though gathering herself. "It was a couple of years ago. He died in a car accident."

"Dammit! My father died in a car accident too," I confide, knowing what she must be going through.

"You'll have to excuse me," she says, heading for her

van, "I've got some business to take care of." She pulls a cell phone out of her pocket on the way over.

When I get home Stu confronts me. "What are you gonna do about it?"

"About what?" I say.

"About the TOX thing," he says, as though I should know.

"I don't know yet."

"I been thinking about it," he says. "Maybe you should sue 'em."

"Maybe," I say. I could contact Frank Hendrickson, a lawyer from Prince Albert I know, have him look into it. But what I really want to do is set the record straight. So, instead of calling a lawyer, I call CBC TV.

"I want to make a statement," I say to the reporter who covered Lionel's memorial.

"Yes?" he says.

"That the TOX report was all fabrication and I did not say there was a fifty-fifty chance that a farmer murdered Lionel Morrison."

"But you did say it."

"I did not. They doctored the tape," I say, irritated.

"I'll talk to my producer," the reporter says, "see if we can get you on tonight's six o'clock news."

"I'd sure appreciate it. I don't want the farmers to think of me that way."

"It may be too late for that," he says. "I'll get back to you."

I make my way down to the bear pit, my office in the basement or lower level, as Rosie likes to call it. Several voicemail messages blink on our business line. More evidence that I haven't paid any attention to business since all this happened.

We have one last fishing party coming to the lodge before freeze up, which means we'll have to head up north right after the wedding. I confirm the booking with our Dallas rep and then spend a couple of hours paying bills and sending out thank-you cards to our guests.

As I push back from the desk, the answering machine blinks at me insistently. I hit play. The first message is reminding me that I have yet to take advantage of the great features my credit card company is offering in its latest ploy to suck more money out of me. I hit erase before its finished. The second message is an inquiry from a travel agent regarding availability at the lodge next season. I wish I could respond, but we still don't have our lease. Sixteen years in the business and now it's one year at a time. The government would really prefer to give the land to a big mining company. When message three begins it's like hearing the voice of a ghost.

Hello, Bart, it's Lionel. We've got the propane tank and we'll be over in a few minutes. Can't cook a steak without fuel, can you? Talk to you soon.

Propane tank? What the hell's he talking about?

As I step out the front door, Rosie drives up in her

van. Her new hairdo is beginning to look a little less like a mop, or maybe I'm getting used to it. She halls a humongous art portfolio and easel up the front steps.

"What are you doing out here?" she says.

"Oh, just taking some air," I say, breathing deeply. "It's clearing up."

"Yeah, now that I'm finished painting. Where's Annie?"

"She and Emma are having a snack."

She gives me an undecided look. "Okay, what are you really doing out here?" She can always tell when I'm lying. It's what keeps me honest.

I hold up the answering machine cassette tape. "There's a message from Lionel on this."

She looks at it, a troubled expression on her face. "What's the message?"

"It doesn't make a lot of sense."

"Why do you say that?"

"He says he's bringing over a propane tank for the barbecue."

"What?"

"I know. What would he be doing with a propane tank? And he says 'we' like there's somebody else with him."

"Who would that be?"

"Exactly. Who would that be?"

Rosie pushes by, as if anxious to get past me, the message on the cassette, and the person who was with

Lionel when he made that phone call. I hear her gently cooing to Emma, but there's fear in her voice too.

At the police station the detectives are silent as they listen to the tape.

"What do you make of it?" Hutt asks me.

"I don't know."

"Why didn't you bring this in earlier?" Klassen says.

"I didn't listen to my messages until today."

"Why not?"

"It's our business line, and I just haven't paid much attention to it since . . ."

Klassen shows his irritation with a derisive puff of air.

"Is there anything else you haven't told us about?" Hutt says, dryly.

"No."

"You never asked him to bring a propane tank over to your house?"

"Of course not, why would I?"

"Because you ran out of propane," Klassen says.

I shake my head.

"So, why would he be bringing propane to your house?"

"I have no idea."

"Okay," Hutt says, reluctantly. "If you were to guess why he was bringing it, what would you say?"

"I would say somebody told him that I needed the propane."

"And who would that be?"

"The one that's with him when he makes the phone call."

"Okay," Hutt says, "so who is that person?"

I shake my head. "I don' t know."

"Guess," he says.

"I really don't feel comfortable guessing, besides I haven't got a clue who was with him, except it's probably the same person that killed him."

As I leave the RCMP detachment, I feel a need to be at the Wheat Pool grain elevator again. To see what I missed while I was discovering Lionel's corpse. To imagine him once again under that pile of wheat.

When I arrive, George Kostiuk, the grain buyer, is putting away the remains of his bagged lunch. "Hello, George," I say, stepping into his office that's attached to the main elevator.

"Yeah, hi," he says, a little startled. The tidy office is flooded with natural light that comes in through windows on three sides.

"Open Sunday, I see."

"I work when the farmers work. Harvest is going full tilt right now."

"How's it going with the house?" I ask.

"If it were going any slower, it wouldn't be going at all," George says. New to Crooked Lake, George and his wife bought a ramshackle cottage at Ireland's Point that he's converting into a year round residence. "I don't think the wife is too thrilled." He chuckles, though it seems a little forced. They moved to town after his last elevator was shut down. It was the second one the company had closed on him, he told us. "Now, what can I do for you?" he says.

"I'd like to ask you a few questions about that day."

George raises his bushy eyebrows, apparently disturbed by the thought. He takes his time removing his rimless reading glasses. "I wouldn't normally talk about this, you understand?" he says. "But since you found him."

I nod.

"So, what did you want to know?" he says.

"Well, for instance, how did they get into the elevator?"

"Came in through the bathroom window. Broke the window and slid the lock aside."

"No alarm?"

"Not in the can."

"And no motion sensors?"

"Nope. The company never saw the need for it. I mean, there's no cash here, nothing of value really. Maybe the computers."

"So from here there's no problem getting into the main elevator?"

"Just unlock the deadbolt, slide the door out of the way and in you go."

"Was it a busy day?"

"Oh yeah, with harvest and all," he says, taking his dusty cap off and repositioning it on his balding head. "I probably had at least thirty loads come in that day."

"How did the wheat end up burying Morrison?"

"I'll show you," he says. We step into the working area of the elevator and he points to an electrical box with two pushbuttons. A green one and a red one. "This operates the hydraulic up there that opens and closes the hopper." He looks up into the darkness at a funnel-shaped shoot about thirty feet in the air.

"How much does a hopper hold?" I ask.

"A hundred bushels." George twists his head. "That's enough to bury anybody."

He examines his familiar worksite. "I've never had an accident or anyone injured in all the years I've worked in elevators. Except the time a painter fell off an annex, but that had nothing to do with the elevator itself."

I can see the regret on George's face. He isn't happy that his long career will be marred by this horrific incident.

In the parking lot the wind is turning the dust into tiny twisters. I roll up the window and head for White Pine Beach. I want to make sure the gusty winds aren't creating any problems for our airplane that's tied up there at the dock. I'm also thinking that by avoiding my usual coffee-time haunt, I will avoid the media that still pervades the town covering the investigation. I'm counting on that CBC reporter to get my statement on tonight.

The lake has turned a dark blue, reflecting the clearing skies. At the dock, I tighten the ropes that secure the plane, and check the bumpers that protect the floats.

The smell of french fries, onions and vinegar greets me as I enter the beach café. Some travellers have stopped in for coffee. A few smokers dressed in warm jackets sit out on the balcony looking at the white-capped water on the lake. I take a stool at the counter and order a cup of coffee and a giant chocolate chip cookie. I'm chomping away when Reverend Roy walks in looking very pleased with himself.

"Good afternoon, Bart," he says.

And then I see why he's pleased. Enid Pond is with him.

I raise my cup and cookie in a mock toast, my mouth incapacitated.

While chewing, I notice Reverend Roy admiring Enid's backside. She now wears snug jeans and a leather jacket. Her streaked hair is held back by a heart-shaped comb.

"Here you are again," I say, after swallowing my cookie.

"A coincidence?" Enid asks, smiling. "Or something more?"

The reverend doesn't look happy at this exchange.

"Can I buy you a cup of coffee?" I say. "You too Roy," I add, so he won't feel left out.

"We are the ones who should be buying you the coffee," Roy says. "Lord, you're a celebrity. How is it we find you here all by yourself?"

I look away in embarrassment. "Just came out to have a look at the plane."

"You have an airplane?" Enid says.

"Yeah, a Cessna 185, it's tied up at the dock. We keep it here when we're home from the lodge."

"Bart has a commercial pilot's license, you know?"

"You don't say?" Enid looks me over as if re-evaluating.

"So what brings you out here?" I ask.

"We came to discuss a catering job," Roy says, looking over appreciatively at Enid. "The Nagy's sixtieth. The UCWA will do the prep, serving and clean up, while Enid looks after the chefery." Roy smiles at his own cleverness.

We move to a booth at the window and the waitress brings two more coffees. Enid declines my offer of a giant chocolate chip cookie, but Roy accepts one and bites into it enthusiastically.

"So have you learned anything new in the case?" Roy mumbles through his cookie.

"What case?" I say.

Roy looks over at Enid and nods in my direction. "Bart single-handedly brought a murderer to justice only last year." Enid looks me up and down, again re-evaluating.

"They were trying to blame it on a good friend of mine, that's all," I say. "And it was the police that captured the suspect."

"I saw your interview on TV last night," Enid says.

"Yes, wasn't that something?" the Reverend says, betraying mixed feelings.

"Do you really believe a farmer did it?" Enid says, waiting for my response with bemused interest in her green eyes.

I stop and take an exasperated breath. "No, I don't. And by the way, even though they made it look like I said those things, I didn't."

"Speaking of farmers, did you hear about Jerry Harper?" Roy says.

"What about him?"

"Police are looking for him."

"Why?"

"They think he might have something to do with Morrison's murder. Maybe you're right, maybe it was a farmer."

"I am not right. I don't know who did it, and that includes Jerry Hooknose Harper.

"He could have done it?" Enid asks. "From what I hear he's got a real hate on for Sombrero."

"Like they say in the media," I reply, "no comment."

"The media can be a devious bunch," the Reverend says.

"Don't I know it?" I say.

"Sometimes the story needs to be told," Enid says.

"Quite right," Roy says, apparently not wanting to veer too far from Enid's opinion.

"I'm not interested in the media," I say, "with one exception. CBC said they'd let me make a statement, hopefully on tonight's six o'clock news."

"What will you say?" Enid asks.

"Well, I want people to know that the TOX report was media hocus-pocus and that I don't have an opinion on who murdered Lionel." Of course if I were being totally honest, I would include a farmer in the list of those who had a motive to kill Lionel. Sombrero has been snapping up land like a dragonfly snaps up mosquitoes.

As I go up to pay for the coffees, Roy pulls out a clipboard he brought along for the meeting and he and Enid get down to business. I notice they remain sitting next to each other in the cosy booth.

When I get home the CBC reporter and his crew are waiting for me in front of the house.

"We don't have a lot of time," he says, as we enter, "so we'll have to work fast." And away goes the dining room table, out come the sausage-size cables and the location of the breaker box is requested. "So, the way this will go," he says, "I'll introduce you, ask a few preliminary questions and then we'll get into the TOX thing."

Within minutes we're ready to go. We each occupy

one of the tall stools. The lights are warm and bright. The interviewer turns to the camera and in a resonant voice says, "We're here in Crooked Lake, Saskatchewan at the home of Mr. John Bartowski who discovered the murdered body of Sombrero CEO, Lionel Morrison." He turns to me. "Mr. Bartowski, do you believe the murderer is a farmer?"

Is that what he calls a preliminary question? "No," I say, emphatically.

"Then why did you tell Tara Spencer on TOX News that there is a fifty-fifty chance it was a farmer who murdered Lionel Morrison?"

"I did not tell her that."

"Then how do you account for your voice and image?"

"They doctored the tape. Look, do I get to make my statement or don't I?" I say, under my breath.

He gets the nod from the producer. "In exchange for exclusive coverage, CBC is providing Mr. Bartowski with the opportunity to make a short statement."

"To begin, I do not believe a farmer killed Lionel Morrison. And just to be clear, I do and always will support farmers and the farming community. And I deny saying that they were responsible for Lionel Morrison's death. I have no idea who killed him. That I discovered his body may suggest that I have more knowledge than others. That's not the case. What I know, you know. It's all been in the news."

Lionel Morrison's murder and my interview are the third story on the six o'clock news. The first is that a rock starlet with a nice belly button is playing a concert in Saskatoon. The second, yet another politician has been caught with his pants down and his hand in the till. The phone rings off the hook until I turn it off for the night. In response to my appearance on the news most people are supportive, but some are still anatomically inclined.

Monday
September 24th

———————

"Good job on TV last night," Ron Diccum says as we enter the post office together next morning.

"Thanks," I say. It all seems like a blur to me now.

Ron stoops to open his mailbox. Standing six foot six and weighing in at well over three hundred pounds, he is by no means a small fry. He pulls an armload of mail and a newspaper out of a large postal box situated on the bottom row. The headline on the paper reads, *Sombrero Chemicals Kill CEO.*

"Let me see that," I say, almost wrenching the paper out of Ron's hands. I skim the article. "He was sprayed with anhydrous ammonia."

"What's that?" Ron says.

"Fertilizer, it says here."

"Fertilizer? Right from the start people have been saying Morrison was murdered by a farmer, eh?" Ron says. "And who else uses fertilizer but farmers?" He takes back his newspaper and shoves it into a recycled bag with his mail. "It's like you said, they figure a farmer did Morrison in."

"I didn't say that."

"I thought that's what you said."

"That was the whole purpose of my statement on TV last night," I say, unable to hide the irritation in my voice.

"Oh," Ron says, his full lower lip moving upwards as if to engulf his fleshy nose.

A gravely voice says from behind me, "Is that all you got to do is stand around and jaw?" I look down to see René Robert standing there with what look like safety glasses perched on his small bulbous nose.

"New glasses?" I say, trying to keep a straight face.

"Yup, just got 'em yesterday," he says. They resemble two magnifying glasses slung together in a huge black frame. "Got to wear 'em for driving, eh." he says.

"Driving?" I say. "Driving what?" Last year I helped René put his car into storage.

"What do you think?" he says.

"René, there's no license on your car." We got a refund on the insurance, even put the car up on blocks.

"It's stuck in the back window. I got three days for forty-five bucks. With that license and these," he grasps the thick arms of his new glasses with his stubby fingers, "I can get around just like other folks."

I roll my eyes toward Ron who doesn't know the feisty ninety-year-old. This feels wrong in so many ways.

"How about taking me for a ride?" I say.

"Where do you want to go?" René asks."I'll just come along," I say, not adding, to ensure you're not over estimating your newfound visual capabilities.

"I don't want to be treated like some kind of old fuddy-duddy, you hear?" René says in his cantankerous voice.

"I'm doing the best I can," I say, exchanging glances with Ron. "By the way, René, do you know Ron Diccum? Ron is the greens keeper at the golf course. Took over from Nick Taylor."

"I've seen him around," René says. Hard to miss Ron.

"Glad to meet you," Ron says, in his incongruously high-pitched voice.

"Likewise," René replies, frowning up at the huge man who must look massive through the thick lenses. "Well, you want to go for that ride or not, sonny?" he says. "I can't stand around jabbering all day like you fellas."

With his seat adjusted all the way up and forward, René still cranes to see over the steering wheel of the huge automobile. As he pulls away from the curb he overshoots the centreline, just missing an oncoming car, for which he receives a not so friendly frown. René honks back at the poor woman who had skilfully avoided his giant seventy-six Mercury Grand Marquis, one of the biggest boats ever launched during the gas-guzzling seventies. After he's straightened out, René takes a hand off the wheel and reaches for a cigar that sits half smoked in the drawer-sized pullout ashtray.

"Would you mind not smoking?" I say. My look says, lets concentrate on the road.

His look says, don't treat me like an old fuddy-duddy.

René heads south out of town, where it's straight and flat. The grid road is freshly gravelled and dry as a bone.

"Sometimes I dream about drifting along gravel roads just like this," he says, "pulling a plume of dust behind. It's like I could go *anywhere* on that road." A small smile wrinkles his cheek.

Rosie's reaction to René's driving is, "He's going to kill himself or somebody else."

"He promised to stay off the highway," I say, "but insists on driving country roads. Says it feels like freedom."

"Did you see the paper?" Rosie says, nodding toward *the Star-phoenix* that lies on the kitchen table.

"Yeah."

"Fertilizer for pity sake," Rosie says. "Why should fertilizer kill you?"

"God only knows." I think about the picture that Hutt showed me that day. The frost burns on Lionel's face were evidence of what anhydrous ammonia could do to human flesh.

Yelping and scratching at the back door disrupts my thoughts. As I take Butch off the rope for his walk, Annie appears on the deck.

"I'll go with you," she says. "Just give me a minute."

Butch barks excitedly as he races back and forth across the browning lawn. I gaze out onto the stubble field behind our house and look toward the cemetery where my mother and father are buried. It gives me a warm feeling usually, but today a chill runs through me as I think of what happened to Lionel.

Annie has put on the heavy wool pullover that she got in Iqualuit. Her shoulder length hair hangs below a matching toque.

The wind out on the prairie will be stronger than in the yard where our poplar trees are shooting for the sky in a way I never thought possible. We put in two staggered rows of them on the north side to provide shelter from the wind, and block the snow from piling up in the winter. After only five years the trees are already forty feet high and climbing.

It puts me in mind of malignant cells multiplying at a fearsome rate. The cold feeling returns. To put it out of my mind, I ask Annie, "So, how's everything going with the wedding?"

"Fine." Butch darts across our path, panting heavily. "I just wish this murder didn't have to happen in the middle of it." She gives me a little girl look. "Is that selfish of me?"

"Don't worry, Honey, things will die down once all the hoopla's over."

"When's that going to be?"

I give her an uncertain look. "That's hard to say."

"When they catch the guy, right?"

"I guess," I say. I haven't been able to put anything past this kid since she was six.

"How are you doing, Daddy?"

"Well, how do I look?"

"Considering what you've been going through, pretty good. You're still the tallest, darkest and handsomest."

I give her a goofy grin. I decide not to tell her about my health concerns. I don't need to add any more distractions to the wedding.

Annie smiles and puts her arm through mine. "I want you to be careful, though. I want you to be at my wedding to give me away. So don't go doing anything foolish like you did last year."

When I was knocked unconscious, pushed down a deep ravine and nearly killed by a shotgun blast. I have no intention of going through that again. "Don't you worry," I say, "nothing's going to keep me away from your wedding."

Besides cemeteries, Cemetery Road is home to several hobby farms, each with new mini-machinery, brightly painted outbuildings, and a barking dog in the driveway. Butch either ignores the hounds or just does a whole lot of peeing in their direction.

"So, what do you see in your future?" I ask, trying to get off the subject of murder.

"I see Randy and I working together as an environmental team," she says, thoughtfully. "Our specialties, animals and birds, compliment one another. And after the children are a little older, we can work together anywhere in the world."

"Children?"

"We plan to have three."

"Three?" I can't help but grin foolishly and squeeze her around the shoulders as we reach the United Church Cemetery.

We visit Dad's grave. He died when I was five. I don't remember much about him except that he was bringing me home a birthday present when he had the head-on collision at Norman's curve. Mom never really recovered from his death. In and out of mental hospitals, she finally took her own life. Her stone reads, *At Peace in the Arms of the Angels.*

The wind has picked up. Annie puts up her hood. I pull out my cap and roll up my collar and we walk briskly and silently back home.

Randall who just got back from Moose Jaw today is off to Vancouver tomorrow for his job interview. Perhaps as penance for leaving his fledgling family yet again, he volunteers to make supper, assuring us it will fit our routine of a light evening repast. He says it's going to be a green meal too, what ever that is.

Around six-thirty we sit down to a nice stew with lots of garden veggies and plenty of very tender chunks of beef.

"Where's the bread?" Stu says as soon as he pulls up his chair. His ritual is to sit down, grab a slice and apply butter to it.

Annie places a basket of whole wheat bread on the table to which Stu responds with a grunt.

"So, did you hear about Lionel Morrison?" I ask

Randall.

"Yeah," I was listening to it on the radio on the way up," he says.

"That anhydrous ammonia is some dangerous shit," Stu says.

"That will do with the language, young man," Rosie says.

"Why is it so dangerous?" I ask Randy.

"Anhydrous ammonia is a toxic chemical . . ."

"In other words, poison," Stu inserts.

"And because it's dispensed under high pressure," Randall goes on, "it has to be handled very carefully to avoid accidental exposure."

"What if somebody did it on purpose," Stuart says, "like Jerry Harper?"

"We don't know that," Rosie says.

"It's pretty obvious," Stu says. "The guy delivers anhydrous ammonia, right? And now where is he?"

"That's for the police to find out," Rosie says, giving Stu another stern look.

"Is there anything you can do if you get this stuff on you?" I ask.

"Flood the exposed area with water, the colder the better," Randall says. "But it boils at minus twenty-seven degrees Fahrenheit."

"What the hell does that mean?" Rosie says.

"Mom," Stu admonishes.

"It means that human tissue freezes and burns simultaneously when exposed to it," Randy says.

"My god," Rosie gasps.

"I heard it sucks your eyeballs right out," Stu says.

"Don't be silly," Rosie says, while looking at Randall.

"Anhydrous means without water. So it does absorb any moisture it comes in contact with. It would seek out all the moist places on the body," Randall says, "like the eyes, the nose, the mouth . . ."

"The armpits, the crotch," Stu says.

"Stuart," Rosie says.

"But why do they use it if it's so dangerous?" Rosie asks.

"Yeah, what's so great about this stuff?" Annie says.

"When it's injected into the soil," Randy replies, "it sucks up whatever moisture is present and immediately goes to work right at root level. So it's very efficient. It's never exposed to the air and no residue of the chemical is left after only a few days. Also low volume means lower transportation costs and less damage to highways. Some people say it's as green as it gets in the corporate farming world."

"Other than it'll kill you," Annie scoffs.

"Maybe we should get off this topic and enjoy Randy's nice supper," Rosie says.

Randall tells us about the green meal as we enjoy our dessert—Rosie's homemade chokecherry syrup over organic yogurt. "There was nothing on the table that was produced more than fifty miles from here. And no animals died to provide this meal."

"What about the beef?" Stu says, rudely pointing his

finger at Randall.

"There was no beef in the stew," Randall says. "That was tofu."

"Ugh," Stuart utters

"Why no beef?" Rosie says. "It's protein, we need it."

"Raising cattle to eat is extremely harmful to the health of the planet," Randall says. "We can get protein from many other sources, and at a much lower cost to the environment."

To which Stuart replies, "What's going to happen to the cattle farmers if everybody starts eatin' tofu?"

Tuesday
September 25th

———————

At the post office next morning everyone's talking about anhydrous ammonia. Mispronunciations range from anemia to pneumonia. Everyone, too, has his or her own opinion on how Morrison was murdered and even where Jerry Harper might be now. Some think he's long gone, while others aren't so sure.

"Well, where is he then?" Les Thatcher says, anxiously.

"I don't know," Helen Mousie says, "but wherever he is, he better stay there. He won't get far in these parts without being recognized."

"Especially with that mug shot in yesterday's paper," I say. "Hard to miss that face." Jerry's profile photo had been particularly unbecoming, accentuating his gnarly, hooked nose.

Everyone nods in agreement. Surprisingly, it's just then that Jerry's wife, Gail, and her son, come in to pick up the mail. The group clams up as Gail sticks her key into one of the small boxes situated on the top row. She scowls at a couple of bills, and then avoids the group's gaze on her way out. But the boy, about ten years old, looks back and gives me what looks like an entreaty of some sort. I watch him reluctantly shuffle out of the post office.

When I get home, Rosie's expression is grim and there's worry in her eyes. "Dr. Tweenes wants you to call him," she says.

"Okay," I say, "thanks."

"What's it about?" she says.

"Nothing." I gaze down at the mail.

"Don't lie."

I know there's no point putting it off, so I say, "It's probably about the medical I had." I examine her expectant face. "There was a test."

"What test?"

"It's called a PSA."

"What's it for?"

"It's a screening test."

"For what?"

"Prostate."

"Prostate?"

I nod.

"You mean prostate cancer?" Tears form in Rosie's eyes instantly and she comes toward me with outstretched arms, then she hesitates and instead of hugging me she begins to beat on my chest with her fists, saying, "Why didn't you tell me?"

"It's not conclusive," I say, fending her off. "Dr. Tweenes said so. I didn't want to worry you."

"Oh, don't you say that. Don't you dare say that. You know we don't keep secrets from each other. It's not fair." Her clenched fists open and she puts her arms around my neck and pulls me hard into her.

I hold her until she stops shaking.

Prostate cancer can be beaten. At least that's what it says on the brochure at the medical clinic. *Early detection is the key. All men forty and over should have an annual prostate examination.*

When I'm led into the examination room, Doc Chow sits in the one and only chair. "You don't mind if Dr. Chow sits in, do you?" Dr. Tweenes says.

"The more the merrier," I say, hopping up on the examination table and nodding to Ray Chow.

My appointment consists of a little more probing, both into my family history and into my nethermost regions.

"It feels funny," Doc Chow volunteers, rotating his finger a little more vigorously than I would have preferred.

"But that doesn't necessarily signify a problem," Dr. Tweenes says, having had his turn. "That may be it's normal shape."

"It could be BHP too," Doc Chow says, grimacing at Dr. Tweenes.

"What's that?" I gasp.

"Enlarged," Doc says. "But there are no lumps or bumps." Again he tells me to keep breathing.

"That's good, right?" I say, breathlessly.

"Yes," Doc says, though his tone imparts some doubt. But Roger bobs his head positively.

"Do you have any problem urinating?" Doc asks.

"Not generally."

"No sudden urges? Inability to go?"

"Nope," I say.

When the examination is complete and I'm fully dressed once again, I say, "So, what do we do now?"

"We'll get a full blood workup done at the University Hospital," Roger says.

"And if it is cancer?" I ask, boldly.

Neither of them answers for a moment, then Doc Chow says, "Then, we'll see. An oncologist will assess your case and help us determine our next step."

I like that he used the word we. But it isn't really we, is it? It's just me. That's how we come into this world and that's how we go out. The questions I find myself pondering lately are, where do we come from? And, more importantly, where do we go to?

As I sit in my truck contemplating the implications of prostate cancer, trying to reconcile the whole concept in my mind, a face fills my rear-view mirror, scaring the bejesus out of me.

"What are you doing back there?" I yell, opening the door and getting out from behind the wheel.

It's a kid and a friendly looking lab in my truck box.

"You're Jerry Harper's boy," I say. The kid looks a lot like Jerry. Well-shaped head, nice proportions, all but that hooked Harper nose. Poor kid.

His eyes shift away and then all of sudden he bursts into tears. I stand there feeling helpless. The dog licks some tears away and when the kid's down to just blubbering miserably, I put a hand on his shoulder. He composes himself a little.

"So, what's your dog's name?" I say. Perhaps not the most probing question I could ask, but the dog and I wait patiently for his response.

He looks up at me, sniffs, and says, "Happy." But his cracking voice sounds anything but. He rubs tears out of his eyes with the back of his hand.

"That's a good name. So what are you doing back here?" I inquire, gently.

Again his eyes shift. His nose begins to run and he wipes it with his sleeve. But before he can say anything, a horn blares in my ear. It's Gail, driving Jerry's red pick-up.

"Come on," Gail says to the boy, "let's go home."

The kid's eyes seek mine, like he's drowning and I'm a life raft.

"He seems pretty upset," I say.

"He's got something to be upset about, doesn't he? With his dad gone and all." Gail reaches over and pushes the passenger door open.

The dog hops in the box, while the kid climbs into the passenger seat.

"What's your name son?" I say, before he closes the door.

"Jerry," he says, "Jerry Harper, Junior."

"Why'd you get into my truck," I ask, but he doesn't hear me because Gail has already pulled away. Happy's eyes seem to implore me as the truck turns the corner toward the north end of town.

"What did the doctor say?" Rosie asks, when I get home.

"More blood tests at the University Hospital."

"The University Hospital?" Rosie draws out the words like I must have some rare disease that only a scholarly research hospital would dare tackle.

"They just want to verify or refute the findings of the first blood tests. Anyway, that's the next step, and they say my prostate feels funny."

"They?"

"Yeah, both Doc Chow and Roger Tweenes were up there."

"Up where?" Rosie asks.

I tilt my head and frown.

Then she gets it, and rolls her eyes. "What does that mean, funny?"

"An odd shape. But that may be how it is. Though it may be enlarged too."

"Oh, no."

"Well, that's what Doc Chow says.

"Why'd you get the PSA in the first place?" she says.

"It was one of the tests on the medical to renew my pilot's license."

"Thank God for that."

Yeah. Thank God for that.

Since *Tim Horton's* pastries invaded the Junction Stop last fall, trips to coffee row have become dangerous to my waistline. But despite that, it's where you'll find me many mornings or afternoons around coffee time.

Sitting at the counter is Father Lebret, *sans* collar. He's called the Holy Roller, and not for reasons one might expect. I say hello to the father and a few others. Les Thatcher is taking his break from the post office. He often regales us with the latest technological advancements on the stamp-licking front.

I order a half dozen *Timbits* and coffee. As I pop one of the delicious morsels into my mouth, a couple of farmers bob duck-billed caps at one another on a topic that seems to have them both heated up.

"You better damn well do it, before it's too late," one of them says, loudly, his voice a bit whiny.

"You don't know what the hell you're talking about?" the other says back.

Marg Woschuck, manager of the Junction Stop, wades into the bay of the horseshoe-shaped counter and says, "All right boys, can I get you something with that coffee?"

They glance over at her and then go back to their argument at even higher decibels.

"I'm going to have to ask you fellas to keep it down," Marg says, showing a little heat of her own. "What's it all about, anyway?"

The two men look sheepish now, having garnered everyone's attention.

"Neil here says I should sell my farm," one of the duckbills says.

"Well, you should," Neil says, in his insistently whiny voice. "We can't compete. The more land the corporations get, the cheaper they can farm it. A lot cheaper than you or me. And they've got all the makings, don't they?"

"What do you mean by that?" Marg says.

"All the machinery, the chemicals, the terminals, the markets. All they lack is the land, and now they've got that too. You can't compete. I say sell, while they're still paying top dollar."

Neil seems to make some sense and as people ruminate on it I notice, to my surprise, Jack Kolchak sitting at a nearby table wearing his shit-eating grin.

"Bigger is better," Kolchak announces in his precise baritone voice as he gets to his feet. "It's cheaper, more efficient, easier on the environment, and it's good for business."

He takes a seat on an empty stool and nods at me in a more or less friendly manner. "Small farming nowadays," he says to the rapt audience, "is no longer viable. You can't make it without subsidies, wheat boards and a whole lot of whining."

Grumbles roll down coffee row like bowling balls, but Kolchak, obviously a seasoned public speaker, acts as though he hears nothing and says, "It's a good thing when you let the economy do what it wants. No interference. Say Sombrero buys up all the land in Saskatchewan, it's because they can farm cheaper than anybody else, and that translates into lower prices. You want to pay lower prices, don't you?"

A couple of coffee drinkers nod their heads, reflexively.

"You can't control the natural ebb and flow of the economy," Kolchak says, "so you have to know how to float in it. Sure, some farmers are losing their land, but others are walking away loaded down with cash. My advice to you is sell your land and buy shares in Sombrero." People chuckle as they often do when money is mentioned.

"I don't think I know your name," Father Lebret says.

"Name's Kolchak. Jack Kolchak. Regional Vice-President, Sombrero Incorporated."

Surprise and amazement fly through coffee row this time.

"Sombrero stocks are down," somebody says through the din.

"Good point," Kolchak says. Now the grumbling returns.

"You've heard of *buy low, sell high*. Well, here's an opportunity to do just that. Sure stock prices are down, but you know Sombrero's going to keep growing. It has to. So, get on board. With a new CEO it's going to be a better company and more profitable to the shareholders. That could be you."

Kolchak seems to take Morrison's passing as a good thing for business.

"What about land?" Neil's buddy says from down the row. "You still buying?"

"Of course, my friend. It's obvious to us that farming as you once knew it is a thing of the past. We are in a transitional period that will make farming a true corporate enterprise. Let's face it, with billions of Asians and Indians needing energy and resources to fuel their rising economies, and now there are GM crops to die for. Imagine the energy we could produce. The sky's the limit to a smart company. And Sombrero has its sights set on the moon."

"Crooked Lake is a farming community," Father Lebret says in what seems a gentle effort to counter Kolchak's self-serving statements. "What's going to happen to our communities?"

"We will still need farmers," Kolchak says. "Farmers to work the land. Farmers with steady pay checks, health benefits, bonuses. Who's got that now?" He looks around.

"Yes, but if you use the land to grow fuel, who will grow the food to feed the world's hungry?" Father Lebret says.

"The boys in the lab will take care of that too," Kolchak says, looking pleased with himself. "They can make a cow the size of an elephant. You ever seen a carrot that weighs sixty pounds, or a cabbage that's bigger than your bathtub?"

"I'm not sure we were meant to grow such vegetables," Father Lebret says.

"So, what's your game?" Kolchak asks.

Father Lebret answers, good-spiritedly, "I'm a Catholic priest at St. Mary's Church here in Crooked Lake."

"No collar?" Kolchak says, examining Father Lebret's jacket that sports leather sleeves and a number of championship bowling crests.

"Oh, yes," Father Lebret says, a lamenting tone in his voice, as though he's more comfortable without the collar. "They're worn for all sacred occasions, weddings, baptisms, funerals, mass and so on. And where do you hail from?" he asks Kolchak.

"I live in Saskatoon currently, but I go where the company sends me." I notice he's been watching the door closely. "I'm gonna have to cut this short, gentlemen," he says. Getting up, he slings a jacket over his shoulder, drops a few bills on the counter and says, "Have yourselves a good day."

A van pulls out on to the highway a minute or two later. A shiny new mini-van.

When I get home Stuart is watching TV downstairs in the rec room. He's laughing uproariously at a program that has people attempting to do near impossible physical feats while the announcer celebrates the pain of failure in droll tones. As I walk into the bear pit, the phone rings.

Randall's father, Andrew McGregor, is on the line.

"Nice to hear from you," I say, cordially. "Randall left for the coast this morning."

"Yes, we spoke to him," McGregor replies in his Scottish brogue. "Actually he suggested I give you a call."

"Preparations for the wedding are on schedule, though the cost seems to have escalated a little, hope you're okay with that?" I say, all in one breath.

"It's about that I'm calling," Andrew says. "You see, we've run into a bit of a snag here."

"Snag?" I say, sucking in air.

"Yes. I'm afraid a situation has come up which will preclude us from contributing to the wedding."

"Preclude?"

"Yes, if you know what I mean?"

"No, I don't," I say, trying to contain myself.

"I'm afraid I leveraged a good portion of our assets to enter into a particularly lucrative investment that very unexpectedly took a turn for the worse. It required all that we had and more to cover the loss."

I'm speechless, but my mind is screaming, "We're going to have to pay for the whole goddamned wedding now!"

"I suppose you're thinking," McGregor says, "like everyone else, that I'm a rich bloody doctor? The fact is I have extremely high overhead and my expenses have gone through the roof. The only way for me to make money is to invest," he adds, almost defensively. "And sometimes you win and sometimes you lose."

"It sounds extreme to put up everything on one deal," I say.

"Yes, but what a deal had it come through," he says, longingly.

"You'll have to tell me about it some time," I say, trying to keep the sarcasm out of my voice, and in no mood to stay on the line with him any longer than absolutely necessary. "Shall I tell Annie, or will you?" I ask, wanting to rub it in.

"Look, Bart," Andrew says, "we intend to pay you back when we get out from under."

"I'll look forward to that day," I say, with little patience left.

"Our regards to Rosie and Annie," he says in his broadest brogue before hanging up.

"Rosie," I yell, banging down the phone. "Ros-ie," I yell even louder as I head for the stairs. In my haste I trip over the footstool in the rec room and go sprawling on to the floor, but not before stepping on poor Butch's tail, sending him squealing up the stairs. Stu roars with laughter at my slapstick antics.

Rosie meets me at the top of the stairs, "What's all the ruckus about?"

"Stop," I say.

"Stop what?"

"Stop spending."

"What are you talking about? Make sense."

"I just got off the phone with Randall's father."

"Yes?" Rosie says.

"They have a financial situation which will preclude them from contributing to the wedding," I say in a derisive brogue.

"Preclude?" Rosie says. "What does that mean?"

"It means they aren't going to cough up their half."

"Why not?"

"Because Andrew leveraged everything on some investment and now they're flat fucking broke."

"Oh, no."

"Oh, yes."

"Of course," Rosie says, frowning, "that's why they moved to the apartment and are selling their house and all. Poor Randall."

"Randall? We're the ones who are going to pay for this."

"Yes, but it will be hard for him to face us, and Annie too. It's embarrassing."

"They'll survive," I say.

"And we'll manage. Besides this isn't the time to worry about money," Rosie says. "Our only daughter is getting married in a few short days. We'll just have to make due with the current budget, and that's that."

"What budget?" I say.

She gives me an approximative gesture.

I can't help but whimper.

The mail I brought home from the post office is anything but encouraging. A letter from the province gives no response to my application to extend our lease at the lodge. They just keep putting off the decision. The next piece of mail I open is from Canada Revenue Agency. The auditors will be here day after tomorrow.

I phone Larry Ludgate, my accountant, who's flying in from Winnipeg for the audit and coincidently for the wedding. "What time is your flight?"

"I get in to Saskatoon around four," he says. "I should be at your place no later than six."

"Rosie's busy with the wedding," I say, "so don't expect a whole lot of lining up at the trough."

"Don't you worry," Larry says. "And I'd like to help out if I can. Maybe I could tend bar at the wedding or something."

"I need some tough SOB at the bar," I say, "to keep all the drunks in line."

"I can be tough," Larry says.

"Sure you can," I say. "See you tomorrow for supper."

The calendar that hangs next to the phone reminds me it's my turn to help out with the fowl supper ticket sales. The four to six o'clock is considered a plum shift in front of the Co-op Store, as it's usually the busiest. The proceeds of the supper will go to the African village that the town adopted a few years back. It's in Zimbabwe and like Crooked Lake has about a thousand inhabitants. Proceeds from the church's fowl supper can usually support the entire village for two or three months.

I have an appointment at the medical clinic—the blood test results—but maybe by way of delaying the inevitable, I take a short detour to the bakery. As luck would have it, the cops are making a doughnut stop of their own. Fred Snell stands at the glass case perusing the delicacies we're both after. He's not wearing his hat but his close-cropped blond hair retains the outline of the brim.

The baker comes out of the kitchen with a bag of flour over his shoulder. He's dressed in white from head to toe. "Sorry to keep you waiting," he says, slamming the bag down, sending white clouds into the air.

"You must go through a lot of that, eh?" I say, coughing a little.

"No doubt," he says. "I'm usually the one hauling it."

"What kind of flour is it?" I ask.

"Canada Western Hard Red Spring Wheat. The world's best." The exact same wheat under which Lionel was buried. That's one detail the cops did divulge.

Under my breath, I say to Fred, "How're things going in the investigation?"

"How would I know?" he says, as though I'm asking a stone for blood. "The detectives are handling Morrison's case, you know that."

"What about Harper?"

"What about him?"

"Any word on his whereabouts?"

"No."

"Why don't you ask his kid?" I say. "He might know something."

Fred's glare suggests I keep out of it.

My second detour takes me to *the Reporter*. People are generally happy with Dee Elliot, despite or maybe because of her biweekly tirade that she calls the editorial. But you've got to give her credit, she usually lambastes the right parties, at least most folks tend to agree with her opinions. With the exception of those being lambasted, of course.

One of those targets is all too often multinational corporations like Sombrero, Cargill and Monsanto who she says are taking over global food production from seed to feed and devastating the family farm with their GM crops in the process. Jack Kolchak's little discourse back at the Junction Stop was living proof of that.

Letters to the editor in accord with Dee's sentiments have become quite vociferous in their tone, delivering not so veiled threats and even speculating sabotage on these corporations.

"There are some farmers' groups that have really got it in for Sombrero," Dee says. "They think the company is the most aggressive in amassing agricultural land. One U.S. group has even sworn to make an example of Sombrero, so that other agra-businesses will get the message."

"And killing Morrison outside the U.S. would take the heat off of them," I say.

"True. And the way the body was presented, buried under a pile of wheat in an elevator, the most recognized symbol of farming there is. It seems obvious it was done to make a statement."

"I don't know," I say. "But speaking of statements, I just talked to Fred Snell."

"And?"

"He's like a prairie clam. Says Hutt and Klassen are handling the whole thing."

"He's no doubt been told to keep his mouth shut," Dee says. "But I heard they've got a suspect that even Fred Snell wouldn't know about."

"And who would that be?"

"I have no idea, but that's what my snitch heard."

"What snitch?"

"Never mind. What have you got there?" Dee says, eyeing my doughnuts that have already turned the bag greasy.

"You get three guesses, and the first two don't count."

"I just put on a fresh pot of coffee," she says, getting up from behind her desk, a scarred old relic that served her father and editors before that. I take a seat across from her and tell her about Lionel's phone message.

"So," Dee says, "Morrison said he was bringing propane to your house for the barbecue?"

"Yeah."

"You know who uses anhydrous ammonia besides farmers?" Dee says.

"No. Who?"

"Meth labs. They need it to make methamphetamine, i.e. crystal meth."

"You're kidding?" It takes an abomination of chemicals to produce crystal meth Roy said in church. "And they actually use this poison to make the drug?"

"Yup. And you can't buy that stuff over the counter, so usually they steal it from farmers, and what do you think they carry it in?"

"What?"

"Propane tanks. Typically, barbecue tanks."

"Well I'll be damned. That's what must have happened to Lionel then."

"Yeah," Dee says, "especially with that phone message."

"Yeah." And the frostbite on Lionel's face, and the nearly vacant eye sockets.

With thoughts of meth labs running through my brain, my final detour takes me to Lakeview Lodge where I drop off a half dozen doughnuts for René. Actually, three apple fritters, two Long Johns and a Bismarck. René's huge yellow car sits prominently in the residents' lot. I notice he's got a permanent license plate on it now.

With no further detours to take, I make my way to the medical clinic.

As before, Doc Chow attends along with Dr. Tweenes. We meet in Roger's office. It feels a bit crowded in the small room.

"Your blood tests," Roger says, "according to the hematologist, support the earlier high PSA scores. So they've suggested a biopsy," he adds, soberly.

"And is a biopsy conclusive?" I ask.

"As conclusive as you can get without actually removing the prostate and examining it," Doc Chow says.

"I should point out," Roger says, "there have been a few cases where the biopsy led to infection and other complications."

"What do you think, Doc?" I say to Ray Chow.

But Doc defers to Roger. "You're Dr. Tweenes' patient on this. I'm just consulting."

"So, consult," I say.

Doc looks over at Roger, who smiles and nods his assent.

"You could do nothing," Doc says, "and get another PSA and more blood tests in a few months. At the same time we could monitor the prostate to ensure no changes are occurring. We could also start on a course of drugs that have proven to help slow the growth of the prostate. Used in high risk patients."

"Am I high risk?"

"Unfortunately, since your father died young and we have no records of your grandfather, we don't know. But it couldn't hurt in light of the possible BHP."

"No," I say, "I guess it couldn't hurt."

"So, that's the non-invasive approach. But in a man your age, a tumour can grow quickly, so we don't want to take any chances either. The biopsy procedure will take samples of your prostate for external examination rendering definitive proof."

"And how in god's name do they do that?" I say. But I can guess. "So what do you think?"

"Sorry, Bart," Doc Chow says. "That's up to you. Go home and talk it over with Rosie. Look it up on the internet so you know what it's all about."

"When can we do this biopsy?" I say, imagining Rosie's reaction.

"Well, there's a waitlist," Roger says, "but we've got you pencilled in for three weeks from today. If there's a cancellation it may be earlier. Here are your instructions for the procedure." He hands me a photocopied sheet of paper. "Follow them carefully." I shove it in the back pocket of my jeans.

When I arrive home two strangers are sitting in my kitchen, brief cases resting on their laps. They both wear wire-rimmed spectacles and grey suits.

"Hello," I say.

"These folks are from the Canada Revenue Agency," Rosie says. "Mr. Gray and Ms Gray. No relation, they tell me."

The Grays nod in unison, like they've done this before.

"We weren't really expecting you until tomorrow," I say. "In fact my accountant is," I look at the fisheye wall clock, "on a plane from Winnipeg right now."

"We finished our previous audit early," Mr. Gray says, "so we thought we'd get a head start on yours."

Happy days.

Even Rosie's smile is more of a grimace.

"Larry's got the books," I say, hoping that will stop them.

"Then perhaps we can get started on your real assets," Mr. Gray says.

What was it Larry had said not to mention? Damn, I wish he were here.

"Would you care for a cup of tea or coffee before you start?" Rosie says, setting a plate of homemade chocolate chip cookies on the table. It's three-thirty, coffee time in any good bureaucrat's day. The cookies are still warm from the oven, the smell irresistible. Ms Gray does her best to show indifference, but the aroma appears to have Mr. Gray salivating.

He swallows and looks down at his watch, then at Ms Gray. "Please don't take offence," he says, "but you must understand that anything you do or say during this audit will not influence the numbers."

I nod agreeably, but Rosie appears not to be wholly convinced.

Mr. Gray's voice rises and his eyebrows follow as he says, "So, if that's agreeable to you, we would love," he looks at the plate of cookies, hungrily, "to take you up on your offer."

Mr. Gray enjoys a good dollop of cream in his coffee. Ms Gray takes hers black with two sugars.

"What is it that prompts an audit?" Rosie asks, conversationally.

"I'm afraid we can't disclose that information," Ms Gray says, coolly.

"Oh," Rosie says, looking rebuffed.

"What she means is," Mr. Gray says, reluctantly setting down his cookie, "that due to the confidential nature of each tax payer's form, we must maintain a universal code of silence. And while this may sound cold," he glances at Ms Gray, "it's for your own protection as a tax payer."

Exactly twenty minutes and three cookies later, Mr. Gray declares the coffee break over.

They ask me to show them some of my real assets. I almost make a muscle, but think better of it. I lead them outside where they circle my vintage Ford F-100 pickup truck. They take notes and pictures, giving Rosie's van the same treatment. Even Butch's doghouse gets the once-over. All the while their eyes dart here and there, as though looking for something. Something that is, or perhaps isn't there. I hope they don't find it. Or do?

Later, with the smell of fried chicken drifting through the house, I find the Grays both on their cell phones in the living room.

"Would you care for a drink before supper?" I ask, after they've ended their calls. Over coffee and cookies, the Grays accepted an invitation to stay for supper. With the same proviso they invoked earlier. "It won't influence the numbers." But I know they have yet to convince Rosie of that.

Ms Gray has opened the collar of her blouse and removed the ascot she was wearing. Her throat is long and quite lovely. Even Mr. Gray loosens his tie a notch and sets his briefcase on the floor, but still within reach. We are expecting Larry for supper, but since he's yet to arrive, I offer the Grays another cocktail.

Mr. Gray holds up his palm and says, "One's my limit."

But Ms Gray, her hair now hanging about her face and the second button on her blouse undone, says, "Yeah, I'll have another."

A scolding glance from Mr. Gray bounces right off her flushed face. I hand her another gin and tonic and she smiles, not at all like an auditor.

"Supper's ready," Rosie says, leering at me.

I usher the Grays into the dining room. They join Annie and Emma at the table. Stuart comes in and gives Ms Gray an approving glance.

"Oh, what a cute baby," Ms Gray says, looking at Emma who zeros in on the tinkling ice cubes in Ms Gray's drink. Mr. Gray is lost in the fried chicken 'n taters. Somehow the glass stays upright. The ice tinkles. Then the phone jangles.

"I'm stuck in Regina," Larry Ludgate tells me. "Mechanical problems. These damned airlines. I'll rent a car, but I won't arrive until late tonight," he says, without much joy in his voice.

Before I know it, he's hung up, and I forgot to ask him what it is I'm supposed to mention. Or is it *not* to mention.

The Grays knock on our door at precisely one pm the following afternoon.

Ms Gray once again has her hair in a bun. She wears a fresh ascot and starched white blouse. Mr. Gray has a determined look on his face and appears not to be swayed by the mile high lemon meringue pie that rests on the counter.

The dining room table affords the best and roomiest surface on which to spread out the account books for the work ahead.

"It's come to our attention," Mr. Gray says, "that you are about to close and conclude your business, Stuart Lake Lodge. Is that correct?"

"No, it is not correct," I say. "Who told you I was going out of business? Was it the government? They're the ones trying to put me out of business," I say, perhaps more emphatically than necessary.

"We'd also like to examine receipts from your Cuban trip," Mr. Gray says. "What business were you conducting there?"

"I was presenting to a group of potential clients," I say, looking over at Larry.

"I thought most of your clients were Americans."

"I can explain that . . ."

"And the expense claims on your Cessna 185 that carries no passengers . . ."

"It's for emergencies." I look over at Larry again.

The phone rings. And rings. Finally it stops. A moment later Annie shouts down the hall, "It's for you, Daddy."

I excuse myself, to the displeasure of all concerned, though Larry looks relieved to be off the hook for a moment. When I return to the dining room it's only to inform them that they will have to carry on without me. Larry looks panicked. The Grays annoyed. Rosie follows me into the bedroom.

"Where are you going?" she says.

"The university hospital has a cancellation and if I can get there by three, they can do the procedure today." I sit down on the bed to put on my leather walking shoes.

"What procedure?"

I exhale. "A biopsy."

"And when were you going to tell me about this? After it was all over?"

"I'm sorry. I'm just trying to protect you." I look into Rosie's eyes and see the worry there.

"I want to know the truth," she says, "that's all."

"You'll be okay here with Larry," I say.

"Larry?" Rosie says. "Forget that, I'm going with you."

"We need one of us here," I say.

"Well it's not going to be me," Rosie says, "and that's all there is to it."

Leaving the Grays in Larry's anxious hands, Rosie and I cruise into the city in just under an hour. At the university hospital we're directed to the waiting room where, along with a number of others, we wait. A half hour later, a white-coated technician comes out, and examining a clipboard, calls out, "Bartowski?"

"That's me," I say, raising my hand.

"Your bowels are clean?" he says, looking at his clipboard.

Everyone in the waiting room waits for my response. I'm puzzled by the question.

He finally looks at me. "Did you do the cleansing?"

"What cleansing?"

"Oh for god's sake," the technician says, putting his clipboard under his arm and turning, as if to leave.

"Excuse me," I say. "I don't understand." Everyone looks over at the tech for an explanation.

"I suppose nobody told you to do a cleanse before the test?" he says, as though there's no doubt in his mind that I was told.

"That's right," I say. And then I remember the photocopied sheet Dr. Tweenes gave me, still in the back pocket of my jeans. "But I just got a call, like two hours ago, to come in. I didn't have time to do a cleanse. Did I?"

"Okay," the demonstrably beleaguered techie says, "hold on a minute."

When he returns, he tells me that there's been some kind of mix up, no fault of his own, and I'll just have to reschedule the appointment. "And this time clean your bowels," he concludes, peeling the top sheet off his clipboard and crumpling it up.

"Thanks for nothing," I say under my breath as Rosie and I exit the office. One of the other waiters nods in agreement.

"Didn't they tell you?" Rosie says.

"Like he said, there's been a mix up," I say. I don't admit to receiving the photocopied sheet from Dr. Tweenes. "But what a pain in the . . ." And then I think better of saying where.

"Why don't we stop in at Enid's office while we're in town," Rosie says. "We can confirm the menu and drop off a cheque. Might as well do something while we're here. No use the whole trip being a waste of time." She gives me an annoyed glance.

The slice of pie logo graces the large front window of *City Catering and Banquets*. It's located in a strip mall of similar units, housing everything from a vitamin wholesaler to a custom countertop manufacturer.

When we enter the front door, we find Enid sitting at a table that's haphazardly set with various place settings that have been pushed aside to make room for two cups of coffee. One in front of Enid, and the other between the outstretched hands of Jack Kolchak.

"Well, hello," I say, looking from Enid over to Jack.

They return my surprised gape with one of their own.

"I wasn't aware you two knew each other," Rosie says.

"No?" Enid says, swinging her long, skirted legs out from under the table.

"Enid did some catering for Sombrero," Jack says, clearing his throat. "I was just settling up."

"Well isn't that a coincidence," Rosie says. "You know she's doing my daughter's wedding?"

"Yeah, she did mention that," Kolchak says, looking over at Enid, who avoids his eyes.

If I were to describe it, the two of them are acting like teenaged lovers who've been caught in the act by their parents, the musky scent still thick in the air. I wonder what it is that's making them so uncomfortable.

"Was there something I could help you with?" Enid says, finally taking on a more professional manner.

"Yes," Rosie says, "we thought since we were in town, we would just confirm the menu. Make sure we've got all the changes, etc. and to give you a cheque, of course."

"Okay," Enid says, "just let me get your file."

She rises from the table and goes into the back where a small, windowed office contains a desk and file cabinets. Kolchak takes a sip of his coffee, which appears to have gone cold.

"I was wondering," I say to him, "what happened to Chas? Is he still around?"

"Not as far as Sombrero is concerned," Kolchak says. "He got fired."

"Oh, that's too bad."

"I don't think so. He got what he deserved. After all, he didn't do his job, did he? In fact he might even be considered a conspirator according to the police. But he's still around. I saw his ugly mug the other day."

I can't help but wonder, what would have happened if Chas had not stayed at the motel to watch the Yankees play? Would Lionel be alive today?

"So, did you find that Enid did a good job for you?" Rosie asks Kolchak, as though checking a reference.

"Oh, yes. We were very happy with her. And she cooked wheat free meals for Lionel. Some of his meals looked better than mine."

"And how did you come across *City Catering*?" Rosie says.

"I was actually out golfing one day and I ran into Enid in the clubhouse. She gave me her card." He glances at Enid in her office. "And one thing led to another."

I can only imagine. "She's some golfer," I say.

"How would you know?" Rosie says.

But before I can answer, Enid returns, holding a couple of file folders. "I guess we're done," she says to Kolchak.

"I guess we are," he says, and leaves rather reluctantly.

Enid joins us at the counter where she opens one of the file folders. After confirming all the details, we make out a cheque for half the catering bill. It almost makes me weep, knowing we will have to cover the other half after the wedding.

When we get home Larry is asleep on the couch, an empty bottle of scotch on the coffee table next to him. Most of the mile-high lemon pie is gone too. I hope it's a good sign on the tax front.

Some consolation for the day is we're invited out for supper. Larry's invited too, but it looks like he may be down for the count.

As we get ready to go, I'm trying my best to avoid Rosie so she won't try to dress me up for *the occasion*. After all, it's just a night at friends we've known all our lives. What would be appropriate attire?

"Certainly not what you're wearing," Rosie says, predictably.

"I dress up for weddings and funerals," I say, slipping into a comfortable plaid shirt.

Wilma and Nick Taylor's house hides behind a tall caragana hedge. Amber coach lights on either side of the front door welcome us. It looks like they've really put on the dog for the occasion. Nick is wearing good slacks and I think I even detect a hint of aftershave. Wilma wears a skirt with a deep slit up the side and her award-winning legs make frequent appearances.

There are candles burning on the mantelpiece, Willie Nelson's voice drifts through the room and I detect the tantalizing aroma of roasting meat. A good meat course is a badge of honour in the prairies.

"It's too bad Larry isn't coming," Wilma says.

"He had a hell of day with the auditors," I say, not wanting to tell them that we left him passed out on the couch.

"Son's-a-bitches," Nick says.

"They're only doing their job," Rosie says.

"I don't mind paying taxes," Nick says, "but the government just pisses it all away."

"This is not the time, Nick," Wilma admonishes. "You know what we talked about."

"Okay, okay." Then he says, "Wilma invited Ron Diccum, so she made a whole mountain of food." Nick can't help himself.

"We even have Dee Elliot coming," Wilma says, "and you know how she is when it comes to social occasions."

There's that word again.

"What'll it be?" Nick says, offering drinks.

The pair of pants I wore, Rosie described as juvenile.

"I'll have a white wine," Rosie says.

The shirt dated.

"I'll take a beer," I say.

And the jacket ridiculous, but I refused to change, so she finally gave up.

Ron Diccum arrives a few minutes later and sits across from Rosie and me, filling the other side of the room.

This leaves little space for Dee when she arrives and squeezes in next to him on the four-seater couch. Dee wears black slacks and a long white shirt that hangs almost to her knees. She has a string of chunky red beads around her neck that match her red-rimmed glasses.

"So," Nick sets a litre of beer in front of Ron, "how're things going at the golf course?" Nick's interest is more than casual. Ron took over when Nick was fired as head greens keeper last year.

"Oh thing's are good, real good . . . yeah, yeah," Ron says in his high-pitched, breathy voice. When no one else says anything, he says, "Yup," in a final affirmative. Then he takes a huge swallow of his beer, draining half the stein.

"Jeez, when I worked there, I always had something to bitch about," Nick says.

"You've always got something to bitch about," Wilma says. "Would you give it a rest please?"

Cupping his mouth as if to keep it hush-hush, Ron says, "Except some of them board members are real winners, eh?"

Nick doesn't need to be reminded. "Know exactly what you mean," he says, "same bunch of assholes they always were."

"All right," Wilma says, by way of averting Nick's well-worn tirade on the subject. "We have some nice *hors d'oeuvres* for everybody." She sets down a large platter filled with cut vegetables and smoked oysters on star-shaped crackers. Next to those she places some napkins. But it isn't until Rosie comes out with a heaping platter of hot chicken wings and Wilma the three kinds of sauce that we dig in.

Wilma has indeed laid on extra to ensure Ron won't go hungry. He looks content, chewing happily, ignoring the sauce that's smeared across his chin and the back of his hand. He drains his beer stein, then says, as though no time had elapsed, "The only other thing I got a problem with is that slough over by the driving range."

"Dugout," Nick says.

"What?" Ron asks.

"It's not a slough, it's a dugout."

The phone rings, interrupting the gripping conversation. Wilma tells Nick to ignore it. But after a full minute of ringing, he sighs and picks up the phone.

"Hello. Yeah, she's here. Hold on."

"It's for you," he says to Dee who peers at the phone, a perplexed look on her wide face. She takes the receiver and goes into the foyer where she has a short conversation with the caller. When she returns a few minutes later she apologizes for the interruption.

She looks at me and says, "They found the propane tank."

"What propane tank?" Nick says.

"The cops think the anhydrous ammonia that killed Morrison was transported in a propane tank," Dee says. "Now they've found it. And it's half full of the stuff."

"Where'd they find it?" I ask.

"Dumped out behind the Esso station," Dee says.

"And they even know who the tank belongs to."

"Who?" Wilma says.

"Jerry Harper."

"Well, that's it for him," Nick says, with finality.

All at once big Ron puts a hand to his throat and irrupts from his seat, knocking over the coffee table, *hors d'oeuvres* and all.

"He's choking on one of them damn chicken bones," Nick shouts.

Ron's face grows flushed and his eyes look like they're about to pop.

"Give him the Heimlich," Rosie cries out.

I get behind Ron and try to put my arms around his midsection. My hands don't even come close to joining. Nick comes up in front of Ron and grabs my hands. We do our best to give him a tag-team Heimlich manoeuvre. Nick resorts to shoulder blocks at one point, and sure enough, out pops a chicken wing. A look of utter amazement washes over Ron's face as he falls heavily onto the couch and reaches for his puffer.

After Ron has caught his breath, he retreats to the bathroom to clean up, while Wilma removes the flying chicken wing and Rosie and Dee help clean up the mess.

Over coffee and homemade chocolate swirl cheese-cake, I realize that it was when Jerry Harper's name was mentioned that Ron choked on his chicken. Does Ron know something? Or was it just his gluttoness eating habits? Wilma prudently sends the remaining chicken wings home with Dee, while Ron looks on hungrily.

The following morning at coffee row the discussion turns to the subject of murder.

"I heard that maybe he didn't die right there at the elevator," one coffee drinker says.

"You don't say?" Bill Bird, the retired English teacher, says with some interest.

"Why didn't they say so in the paper then?" asks the gas jockey, whose overalls are fouling up the place.

"It seems they're not telling all," Bill says. "Bart, what have you heard?"

"Not a hell of a lot," I reply.

"Oh, come on Bart, you must know something," Bill says.

I look around at the expectant group, and knowing it'll come out soon anyway, repeat what I heard the night before about the propane tank, leaving out the detail that it belonged to Jerry Harper.

"Barbecue tank?" the gas jockey says.

"Yeah."

"Half full of this fertilizer? The stuff that killed Lionel Morrison?"

"Yes."

"So I guess it could be considered the murder weapon," Bill says.

"That's right," the gas jockey says, his eyes squinting.

There's silence for a few moments, some heads twist and some "Yups," are said.

"Despite this tragedy," Reverend Roy says, trying to steer things out of the negative, "we have so much to be grateful for."

"I sure can't complain," the gas jockey says. Automotive emanations waft my way. "Got enough to eat, nobody bothers me in particular, my kids are all but growed up, I got this here job, and I got you fellas." He produces a gap-toothed grin. "What more could a guy ask for?"

Laughter follows the guileless oration.

"Now you may not want to complain," Bill Bird says, "but you have to admit there're some things need settling. We've had a murder, and not just any murder. The whole world is watching. Well, look at Bart there, he's getting all the glory, isn't he?"

"A household name practically," someone says, and others nod and grunt in agreement.

"They interviewed me the other day," Bill says, with timing honed in the classroom. "Wanted to know who I thought killed Morrison. I guess they know I have the pulse of the community, being an educated observer and a chronicler of our town's people and history. You may not have known that I am putting together an historical piece about Crooked Lake. Bill Bird came into this world as Bizliscky Brechuckoffsky. In accordance with family tradition he was given his grandfather's

Christian name and a surname that combined the two family names. You could hardly blame him for changing it, yet he was always looked upon slightly askance for having done so. The Crooked Lake School District hired him, and here he stayed for his entire thirty-five year teaching career. Generations of Crooked Lake kids learned to make birdcalls in Bill's honour.

"Sometimes it's hard to tell the wheat from the chaff," someone says. There are a few sniggers at Bill's expense as coffee time comes to an end.

Out in the parking lot, I wonder if it *was* Jerry Harper who filled his propane tank with anhydrous ammonia and sprayed Lionel with it. He was mad as hell at Sombrero, no question about that.

After a solitary dinner—where is everybody?—I head down to the liquor store to pick up the booze for the wedding. Two hundred and fifty guests are coming to celebrate Annie and Randall's nuptials. We've ordered forties of rye, vodka, rum, scotch and a whole shit load of beer. Then there are ninety bottles of wine for the supper and of course the champagne that Annie expressly requested for the toasts. Fortunately any leftovers can be returned for a full refund. Fat chance, Saskatchewan people come to weddings thirsty.

"May I see your special event permit?" the pretty young cashier at the liquor store says. I hand it over. She trains her eyes on her computer screen and begins pecking away at her keyboard. Finally the cash register whirrs, taps, clatters and rolls.

A couple of young men, bursting out of denim, enter the liquor store and go straight to the back shelves where cases of beer line the wall.

The cashier looks the two men over with unmistakable interest. "Are you taking this order with you?" she asks me.

"Yes, I am," I say.

The young, jean-clad bucks each grab a couple of cases of long necks and carry them over to the counter where the cashier smiles bashfully at them as she rings in my order.

With a final rapid fire series of punches at the machine, she says, "That'll be three thousand four hundred and fifty-one fifty."

"Three thousand . . ." I say in disbelief.

"Four fifty-one, fifty," she says, her eyes alert to the two strapping young men, one of whom wears boots and a ten gallon cowboy hat.

"Right," I say, clearing my throat. When she hands me the printout I look it over. "This can't be right, we didn't buy wine for thirty bucks a bottle."

Looking over her copy, she says, "Twenty-nine ninety-five for the bubbly."

The young men are lined up behind me, and while I'd like to look the bill over more closely, I feel a palpable push to move on.

The tall, skinny manager of the store comes out of his glassed in office to help load the order. "If you want to bring your truck around we can load it through the back door," he says.

The booze, when loaded occupies much of the truck box, leaving only a couple of feet of space at the back near the tailgate. I cover my precious cargo with a canvas tarpaulin. No need to put temptation in people's way. I stop in at *the Reporter*, in this case the Sears outlet, to pick up Stuart's rifle. It comes fully assembled in an easily identifiable box.

After securing the twenty-two behind the seat, I walk down the street to Woslewski's Home Hardware Store. The proprietor, Len, opens the glass case behind the counter with a key that hangs with a dozen others on a chain attached to his belt loop.

"What are you after, Bart? We got .22 longs, shorts, high-powered, hollow point. Whatever you need."

"Better just give me a box of shorts," I say, not wanting to put anything more lethal than necessary in Stuart's hands. "And some 30-30 soft-points as well."

"Right you are," Len says, handing me a small box containing fifty tightly packed .22 calibre bullets and a considerably larger box of 30-30 shells.

The Harper kid has been on my mind ever since he and Happy magically appeared in the back of my truck, so I drive over to their low-rent, two-bedroom bungalow on the north side of town. I pull into the driveway and park behind Jerry's red pickup. A low hedge separates the yard from the street. A kid's mountain bike and a gas barbecue—tankless—huddle next to the house. The scruffy yard looks like it's been left to fend for itself. When I knock on the front door, Gail opens it, but not enough to let Happy out.

"What do you want?" she says, her questioning frown a less than friendly welcome.

"I just wanted to say hello to Jerry Junior," I say.

"Well, I'll pass that on."

"I'd like to say it in person, if I may?"

"We're kind of busy right now." Her eyes express what looks like anger mixed with fear.

"It'll only take a minute," I say.

She throws open the door. "Come in then, if you must."

Jerry Jr. is sitting at the kitchen table. He looks the furthest thing from happy. The dog trots over and sits on its haunches next to him.

"Have a seat," Gail mutters, indicating a chair.

I pull out a spindly wooden kitchen chair and sit down. There are three water glasses on the table and evidence of a recent meal.

"How're you doing?" I say to Jerry in a way that invites a response.

His doleful eyes avoid mine. "Fine," he says, but then he purses his lips and makes an effort not to break down.

"You don't look fine," I say. The boy's eyes are red, his nose is runny and his small hands move about fitfully.

Gail steps behind his chair and rests a hand on his shoulder. "He's fine," she says, "given the circumstances."

"I was wondering what made you hop into the back of my truck yesterday?" I say.

Jerry looks up at his mother, then his eyes momentarily find the ceiling. "Nothing," he says.

"It must have been something," I say.

Again the boy looks at his mother. And as he does I hear a squeak from somewhere above us.

Gail looks around nervously. "We got rats in the attic," she says.

"Big ones," I say.

"Yeah," she says.

There's no more noise from up above, but both Gail and Jerry take furtive glances at me as if to ascertain if I'm paying it any more attention.

I decide to lay it on the table. "Jerry, do you know where your dad is?"

Jerry's red eyes again find the ceiling. "No," he replies, almost as though it were a question.

"Do you know where he is, Gail?"

"No, I do not," she says, firmly, as if to reinforce Jerry Junior's tentative response.

"Are you sure?"

"Yes, I'm sure."

"I guess you've heard how Lionel Morrison was killed?" I say.

"Yes."

"Do you think Jerry could have had something to do with it?"

Though she doesn't look entirely convinced, she says, "No. There's no way."

And just as she says it, there are more squeaks and movement coming from the attic. Now we all look up.

"What's that?" I say.

Neither of them responds.

Now there's a sound of scrabbling on the outside of the house.

I get up and turn toward the door. Gail blocks my way.

"Move," I say to her.

"No," she says.

"Mom," Jerry Jr. cries.

"No," Gail says, forcefully, almost to herself.

"Jerry's out there, isn't he?" I say.

"He didn't do anything."

"Then why's he hiding?"

"You know damn well they're blaming him. Everything points to him."

"But running won't help. He can only prove he's innocent if he turns himself in."

"He's right, Mom," Jerry Jr. says.

Gail stands there resolutely. Tears flood her eyes and Jerry Jr. runs over and puts his arms around her waist.

I push past them to the door. When I get outside, I rush to the side of the house to see if I can spot Jerry. When I don't see him I circle behind, running across the strip of lawn at the back, almost decapitating myself on the clothesline. It's just then I hear a motor start up. When I get to the front yard, it's *my* truck that's speeding away. Obviously he couldn't get out with me parked behind him and like the trusting soul I am, I left the keys in the ignition. With three thousand, four hundred fifty-one fifty worth of booze in the back. Not to mention Stuart's new *Winchester* rifle. Rosie's going to love this.

Gail and Jerry Jr. now stand on the front stoop.

"Give me the keys," I say to Gail.

She looks unsure.

"Give me the keys to the truck," I shout.

She goes inside and a minute later emerges with the keys to Jerry's truck.

"Now, call 911. Tell them what happened."

I hop into the truck and fire up the engine. As I back out, Gail holds Jerry Jr. close to her, making no move toward the telephone.

When Jerry left he headed east toward the lake. I burn some rubber. Jerry's truck moves a lot quicker than mine and before long I'm out of town and following a dust trail that I assume is Jerry. At the railway track the assumption is confirmed when I see a couple of cardboard beer boxes in the middle of the road, oozing foamy suds. I wince at how much it's going to cost me to replace the booze.

A thick dust trail obscures the road, but a mile down

it appears that Jerry has taken a turn north onto another grid road. About four miles later, the dust trail begins to thin out, and soon I see my truck pulled over to the left side of the road next to a considerable sized bush. One that would provide good cover.

I pull up behind my truck, get out and look inside the cab. As I expect, it's empty and the keys are gone. I turn my attention to the bush and try to spy some sign of movement. None is evident. I consider going in after Jerry, but then realize that it's not Jerry I'm after, but my truck and it's cargo.

Hoping there aren't a lot of broken bottles, I turn to the tailgate and pull the tarp back. And just as I do, Jerry irrupts from under it and gut punches me with such force that I collapse onto the ground, uttering, "Uh-uh-uh," while he hops into his truck and reverses out from behind mine, "uh, uh, uh." The sound of his truck dissipates, leaving only the rustle of leaves in the trees and my own breathless utterances.

After what seems an eternity, air begins to return to my lungs and the ghastly pain in my solar plexus subsides a little. I'm a long way from getting to my feet, but at least it no longer feels like I'm going to die. I gulp air greedily as the spiky, dead grass on the side of the road prickles my nose.

The nauseous feeling is going away, though it's being replaced by buzzing in my ears. The buzz becomes a crunch and I realize it's tires on gravel. Big tires coming straight for my head, a little stubby guy behind the wheel, the sun reflecting off thick eyeglasses.

The car comes to a stop inches from my face. A minute later René Robert stands over me, bent at the waist, hands on his knees.

"You all right?" he says.

"Do I look all right?" I groan, spitting gravel.

"What the hell happened?"

"Don't ask."

"Can you get up?" René says. "Here, let me give you a hand." For a ninety-year-old, short guy he's damn strong. He hauls me to my feet and after a few deep breaths I manage to remain upright by leaning on the fender of the car.

"What happened to you?" René says.

"I got sucker punched."

"You did? Who done that?"

"Never mind," I say, "we've got to get moving."

I hold on to the aerial for support. On my way to the passenger door I'm forced to make a pit stop, leaving most of my solitary dinner behind.

"Where are we going?" René says.

"Just go straight, I say, unwrapping a stick of gum. "We'll see if we can spot him."

"Who?"

"Jerry Harper."

"What the heck's going on?"

"I'm not sure. Could be he murdered Lionel Morrison."

"Well, let's not stand around jawing about it then," Rene says.

The big car floats along the gravel road so smoothly that I can almost understand why they would design a car like this. René rides it like a cowboy on a big stallion. His left hand holds on to the steering wheel while his right rests easily in his lap. A small-brimmed straw hat sits jauntily on his round head.

As we go up and down a small hill, my nausea returns, but I tough it out with some more deep, long breaths. I focus on the horizon and my stomach responds positively, so I continue to stare at it. And as I do, I realize I'm seeing a vehicle on the next grid over, putting it exactly two miles away. From that distance all I can see is a red dot, followed by a trail of dust. I tap René on the shoulder and point. He speeds up. I close my eyes again.

René is really moving now. I can't see the speedometer, but I can feel the speed of the big car, the engine with enough horsepower to pull four hundred plows.

When I open my eyes we're gaining on the vehicle that I can now see is undoubtedly Jerry's red pickup.

We near a crossroad just as Jerry does.

"What should we do?" René says through the side of his mouth. The other side is crammed with an unlit stogie. When I don't respond, he asks, "Straight?"

"Let's wait and see which way he goes," I say.

"Then we'll run the bastard down," René says, chuckling to himself.

"Let's just keep him in sight," I say, calmly. But without further consultation, and even less warning,

René takes a tire-tearing turn toward the grid road that Jerry's on. Then he hits the gas and the front end of the car rears up like a bucking bronco, the tail sliding side to side. By the time he's got it under control it's obvious that Jerry has blown through the intersection, not even slowing down.

I give René a baffled glare. His fuddy-duddy look comes out again so I don't say anything.

He manages to keep the car under control, despite the rutted road. It's a secondary connector, and the maintenance too is secondary. All at once the car veers sharply left. René reins it in, riding high in the saddle.

"Try and stay out of those ruts, eh," I say.

"You want to drive?" he replies, without looking at me. I'd love to take him up on the offer, but I don't. He gives me a defiant look and punches in the cigar lighter. The road gets rougher. The lighter pops, and just as he reaches for it, the front right tire drops into a deep rut. The car begins to turn, but continues moving forward as though spinning on its axis. Dirt and gravel fly all around us. René makes a valiant two-handed effort to regain control and with shuddering, grinding and gnashing, the car finally comes to a stop. We hit the ditch, but thankfully we didn't flip over.

I look over at René who's chewed right through his fat cigar. "They should grade these goddamned roads," he says, spitting tobacco.

I cross myself in gratitude that we aren't dead. I did swallow my gum, however. "Good driving," I say, when I catch my breath. René looks at me to see if I'm mocking him.

But it *was* good driving. He kept us from rolling. 'Course, maybe if he hadn't been reaching for the cigar lighter . . .

"I'm sorry I got you into this," I say, feeling awful about putting his life in danger.

"I got me into this," he says. "So don't you worry about me. I'm only sorry we lost the bugger." René resets his eyeglasses on his bulbous little nose, hardly big enough to support the monstrous frames.

The car is sticking out of the ditch on the left side of the road. It takes a lot of spinning and rocking and swearing but we manage to get it out. We check the worn tires and undercarriage but find no real damage.

Naturally Jerry is long gone by the time we get back on the road. René drives carefully, and no cigar.

"We might as well go talk to the police," I say.

René's eyes bulge a little, but he just keeps driving, a slow and steady pace, though he's back to his old habit of one hand on the reins. Eventually we make it safely to the RCMP detachment in Crooked Lake.

Hutt and Klassen are not around, so I sit down with Corporal Fred Snell.

"Okay, so fill me in," Fred says.

"Like I told you at the bakery, the kid, Jerry Junior. He was real upset about something, so I decided to go over to the house and see what was bothering him."

"And?"

"No wonder the kid was upset, turns out Jerry was hiding up in the bloody attic."

"Christ." Fred raises a bushy eyebrow. "And where is he now?"

"I followed him a few miles north of town, but that's the last I saw of him." I decide to keep our little vehicular mishap out of it, but I do describe how Jerry stole my truck and assaulted me.

"So, he's driving his red pickup?"

"Yup."

Fred looks into the outer office. He says to the secretary, Netty Ostrovsky, "When are Hutt and Klassen due back?"

"They're in the city," Netty says, "Supposed to be back first thing in the morning."

"You better get them on the phone," Fred says. A beleaguered scowl appears on his long face. "Looks like it's going to be a long night."

When we pull up to the house in René's car, Rosie frowns at us through the dining room window.

As soon as we get inside, René says, "Found this one lying face down on the side of the road."

"Bart?" Rosie says.

"Thanks René," I say, under my breath.

Rosie gives me an exasperated sigh. "So, what now?"

"Before I answer that," I say, "René and I have to get my truck." I grab the spare set of keys. "It's full of booze, not to mention Stuart's rifle. We'll be right back."

An hour later, with my half-ton parked safely in the garage, I'm sitting at our dining room table eating some of Rosie's genuine beef stew. It feels good to be surrounded by family and friends. René and Larry have joined us for supper.

René grunts contentedly as he brings another spoon full of the thick beef broth to his mouth and slurps, noisily. "So, do you think Jerry Harper done it?" he says.

"It looks that way, doesn't it?" I say.

"Things aren't always the way they appear," Larry says.

"Yeah, just ask an accountant," I say.

Larry gives me a less than professional look.

"I know Jerry's the number one suspect," I say, "but why would he kill Lionel Morrison? He's got nothing to gain by it. And why would he use his own barbecue tank? And the very chemical he delivers?"

"Why'd he take off then?" Stuart says, smearing butter onto a thick slice of bread.

"Good question," Larry says, nodding at Stu.

"And he's not above breaking the law," Annie says. "He was in jail already, right?"

"Yeah, for theft over a hundred thousand," Stu says. "And he's a real asshole."

"Stuart," Rosie says.

"He always was," Larry agrees, "even when he was a kid."

"Speaking of kids," Rosie says, "I feel so sorry for Jerry Junior. Poor little guy's going through a lot."

Everyone nods sympathetically.

"Let's invite him to the wedding," Stuart says, "maybe it'll cheer him up."

"That's a good idea, Darling," Rosie says.

"I better get along," René says, after we've finished off the stew. "For some reason I'm feeling a little tired."

We had a couple of drinks before supper, so Rosie is going to drive René home before going to her UCWA meeting where the fowl supper will be the main topic.

"I don't know what brought you out onto that road today," I say to René, "but thank you for being there."

"I like driving country roads is all," he says. And with that he moves somewhat unsteadily toward the door.

"You haven't forgotten what Saturday is, eh?" Rosie says.

"Wedding bells," René says, jolly with drink and good food.

"And that means all of our attention needs to go to the wedding. From now on," Rosie says, looking in my direction to make sure I get the picture.

"I agree a hundred per cent," I say.

She tries hard not to roll her eyes as she takes René's arm and leads him out to her van.

"Give me a hand with these dishes," I say to Stu as I begin clearing the table.

He gives me his *You talkin' to me?* look.

I laugh, as usual, then point to the pots in the sink.

"Did you pick up my rifle today?" he says, grabbing a dish rag.

"Yeah, I did," I say.

"Well? Where is it?"

"I'm afraid Jerry Harper's got your gun, Son. He must have found it behind the seat." I can see the disappointment in Stuart's face. "I'm sorry, Stu."

"It's not your fault," he says, scrubbing away at the pots. "I just hope he doesn't shoot anybody with it."

Finished clearing the table, I start the dishwasher and wipe down the counters. After sweeping the floor, I find myself pacing up and down, unable to sit still. I can't stop thinking about Jerry, but what can I do?

The phone rings.

"Hello," I say.

"Hello, Bart."

I recognize the Bronx accent. "Is that Chas?"

"Yeah," he says, "I need to talk to you."

"Sure, okay."

"It's important," he says.

"Where are you?"

"I'm on the highway, five minutes from Crooked Lake."

"Do you want to stop by the house?"

"No. How about we meet somewhere else? Someplace private."

Private? What does that mean? I'm still wondering about Chas. Is he really such a big Yankee fan?

"There's a place near you," he says. "Cemetery Road."

Oh great.

"I'll meet you at the Catholic Cemetery," he says.

"Okay," I say, with some reluctance, and hang up.

I realize my truck is full of booze and Rosie's got her van. So how am I supposed to get to the cemetery? Then passing a window I see the solution to my problem. It fills the driveway, all two hundred and twenty-nine inches of it. The keychain with a rabbit's foot on it hangs from a hook next to the door.

I head to the bedroom to change. For some reason I feel like dressing in black.

When I arrive at the cemetery, Chas is sitting in a four-door sedan with a Budget rental sticker on the bumper. He beckons me with a wave and I hop into his rental.

"How you doin'?" he says, sticking out a meaty paw.

"What's up?" I say.

"It's about Mr. Morrison," he says, looking even more brooding than ever.

"What about him?"

"I think I know who killed him."

"Who?"

He turns to face me. "Jack Kolchak. He didn't like Mr. Morrison's plans for the company."

"Even I know that," I say.

"And he's an ambitious son-of-a-bitch. But he's not the only one involved."

"You think there were others from Sombrero?" I ask.

"Yeah. To get control of the company and take it deeper into bio-fuels."

Jack Kolchak definitely championed that philosophy at the Junction Stop.

"Any idea who else might be involved?"

"There's a woman."

"Works for the company?"

"No, she's a caterer. Been hanging around with Kolchak."

"A caterer?"

"Yeah, a real looker too. Long legs, nice chest, streaked hair."

Is he describing Enid Pond, our caterer?

Just as Chas is about to say more, a car flies into the parking lot and slides to a halt next to Chas' sedan. Jack Kolchak jumps out of the driver's seat.

Chas doesn't move, even as Kolchak rips open the door of the sedan and says, "Get the fuck out of the car."

"What's going on?" I say, leaning over Chas to make eye contact with Kolchak.

"He fucking knows what's going on. He's been following me around. Now I decide to do a little following of my own, and he brings me straight to you. Isn't that interesting?"

"Get your hand off my door," Chas says, his voice rocky and menacing.

"Or what?"

"Or I'll break it," Chas says.

Kolchak backs off a little. "Why is it you're following me around?"

"You want to know?" Chas says. "Because I think you murdered Mr. Morrison."

"What? You can't be serious. Why would I kill him?"

"You know damn well why."

"Enlighten me," Kolchak says.

"Kiss my ass," Chas says, slamming the door and starting the engine.

Kolchak bangs on the window with his fist. "You better not be following me around," he shouts.

Chas backs out and peels away, spraying Kolchak with gravel. Without further discussion, he drops me off at home, saying that he'll be returning to the city, and I can get hold of him at the Holiday Inn.

René's car is still at the cemetery, keys in it, but I decide to leave it there overnight. After all who would visit a cemetery at night? After a drink and a sob story from Larry, I retire to what I hope will be a solid eight-hours sleep. But that's not to be. I'm up and down two or three times to pee and to worry about René's car.

Friday
September 28ᵗʰ

On the morning before Annie's wedding, Larry steps out on the back deck as I split some firewood. He stretches his less than athletic body unselfconsciously and puts a crooked grin on his face.

"What happened to our CRA friends?" I ask, after winning the struggle with a truly stubborn piece of poplar.

"Haven't heard," Larry says, reaching for his toes but getting only as far as his kneecaps. "Said they have more questions."

I give him a distracted look.

"So, you still need help at the bar?" he says. "I can handle it. I'll set up. I know all about that stuff and more. I got a bar at home."

I don't need to be reminded. In his five thousand square foot house in a suburb of Winnipeg where he and his two grown-up kids live, his wet bar boasts all that a small cocktail lounge might. And that's the problem. I think Larry has a drinking problem and I don't want it to become Annie's problem on her wedding day.

"Grab an armload, will you," I say, nodding at the freshly split firewood.

Larry follows me back into the house, and after

we've deposited the wood next to the airtight stove, he starts in again about the bar.

I'm saved by the phone. It's Reverend Roy.

"Hello," he says.

"How're you, Reverend?" I say, walking into the living room.

"More importantly, how are you?" he says.

"I'm good."

"I ran into Rosie downtown and she told me what happened. No after effects from that trauma?" he asks, mournfully.

"Well, I wouldn't say that," I say.

"And that's why I'm calling, I thought it would be good to talk it over."

"Oh, yeah?" I say, without much enthusiasm.

When I hang up, Rosie asks for the details.

"Reverend Roy wants to get together. Because of what you told him."

She gives me a questioning look. "What for?"

"I don't know, some sort of debriefing."

"You mean like counselling?"

"No, no, nothing like that. And don't be using that word," I warn her.

"Have you got something to say?" Rosie says.

I make a face. "I don't know."

"I'm glad you're going."

I make another face.

Rosie's mom arrives from Wallburg, the little town a few miles down the highway where Rosie grew up, and takes up residence in the guest room. She feels it's her duty as the only living grandmother to reside with us during her granddaughter's wedding. Some of us agree.

"Want to go for a walk?" I ask Larry. "I need to get René's car."

"Where is it?" Larry says.

"At the cemetery."

"What's it doing there?"

"It's a long story. I'll tell you on the way."

When we reach the cemetery, René's car sits there, window open, keys in it. Everything looks fine, but when I get in, there's an envelope stuck to the steering wheel. On it is printed my name.

I grab the envelope and rip it open.

Don't fuck this up, Bartowski, I read. *Keep your nose out. Or else.*

"Keep your nose out of what?" Larry says.

"If I had to guess," I say tensely, "it would be the murder."

"It's a threat," Larry says. "Who would leave such a note?"

Who would leave such a note? Kolchak? Jerry Harper? Farmers? Drug dealers? Maybe even the police. And what about Enid Pond? And then there's Chas? And any number of others? Maybe the murderer left the note.

All of a sudden Fred Snell pulls smartly into the cemetery lot and comes to a stop next to René's car. He emerges from his blue and white in a cop-like manner, short of sticking his baton into his belt. "What's going on here?" he says, scattering his accusatory gaze over Larry and me.

"Just picking up René's car," I say.

"Why is it here?" Fred says.

"He . . . he couldn't get it started," I say. "I'm not sure what the problem is."

"Give it a try," Fred says in a way that suggests he's willing to lend his expertise to the problem.

When I don't move, Fred says, "I don't have all day."

"Okay, I'll give it a try," I say, sliding in behind the wheel. The envelope sits on the seat beside me.

Before turning the key, I press the gas to the floor in hopes of flooding the engine to justify my excuse for being here. But the big motor ignores my ministrations and starts up without missing a beat.

"Sounds pretty good to me," Fred says, as though we're wasting his time. His shoulder radio squawks. *A red pickup has been spotted.* "I've got to go," he says. You guys just get this car home safely. Looks to me like you're hung over."

"Who? Us?" Larry says, defensively. "No, Sir." He seems to have forgotten passing out about midnight after a remorseful rant about how he'd let his family down.

"Anybody making dinner around here?" Rosie's mom says. "Myra's going to be here soon and we've got to get going on those centrepieces."

"Is there anything I can do to help?" I say. The phone rings and I take it, apologetically. "Hello."

The Grays are coming.

Larry, who's been bunking in the basement bedroom, is out on one of his rambles down memory lane. I hope he won't be too long. The Grays said they'd be here at one o'clock and I don't expect them to be late.

I still have time to meet Reverend Roy at the church for a few minutes. When I arrive, he's sitting in the front pew with papers spread up and down the length of it. He gathers them up and invites me to sit down next to him.

I take a seat and find myself staring at a small bronze sculpture of Christ nailed to the cross. I turn toward the Reverend whose long face seems particularly animated.

"As I said on the phone," he says, "you might like to talk about the incident. It can be helpful to do what's called, *brief therapy*. I've been taking classes at the university so I can keep up with the latest methods."

Just what I need, the latest methods.

Roy nods enthusiastically and says, "Now, tell me, what feelings are you having right now?"

And the session goes down hill from there.

Before I leave, Roy winks at me and says, "You know that caterer of yours is quite the beauty, isn't she?"

"Reverend?"

"Well, she is. And she's turned an eye my way."

"She has, eh?"

"We're going to be working together, and she seems to like me. But she's had a tough go. Her mother left when she was a teenager and she had to look after her younger brother. Her father died of cancer a few years ago," the Reverend says, sympathetically.

"He did?" I say. "Of cancer?"

"He was only fifty-eight."

At home Rosie has prepared a nice tuna salad for dinner. She's trying to lose five pounds over night. Soon after we eat there's a forceful knock at the front door. When I open it, Detectives Hutt and Klassen fill the opening.

"We'd like to ask your son a few questions," Corporal Klassen says.

"What for?" Rosie pipes up from behind me.

"It's about the twenty-two," Hutt says. "May we come in?" The two big men step inside. "We need to get the serial number and verify ownership," Hutt says.

I go to the basement stairs and shout, "Stu."

Of course he doesn't hear me. When I go down, he's under the headphones and I can hear the soundtrack of the video game he's playing. I wonder if he's ever heard of tinnitus.

"Go get the papers for your rifle, Stu" I say. He gives me an irritated look and takes off the headphones. I tell him again.

"What for?" he says.

"Because the police are here and they want to see them."

"All right."

I return to the living room where Rosie is pouring the policemen cups of tea, as though they were guests.

"Just leave my son out of this," I say. "I put the twenty-two in the truck. Stu never even saw the gun."

The doorbell rings.

"Excuse me." Rosie puts down the teapot.

It's the Grays. And Larry's not back. Rosie gets them settled at the dining room table with the promise that I'll be with them directly.

Stuart arrives with all the requisite ownership papers neatly contained in a manila folder. He takes after his mom in the organizational department.

"Thank you," Hutt says to Stu.

"I don't want the rifle," Stu says. There's disappointment on his face.

"I can understand that, son," Hutt says.

Rosie returns to the living room with a harried look on her face. "They're getting antsy," she whispers in my ear. "I've offered them cake, cookies, pie, but they're not biting."

"And a murder investigation cuts no ice?" I hiss back. "Where the hell is Larry?" I make a smiley face at the detectives and say, "You're going to have to excuse me."

Klassen looks bullets at me.

"We have the good fortune of being audited," I say. "The tax folks are waiting for me in the dining room. I'll just be a moment." Hutt only gives me a blank stare.

Finally Larry shows up, having found himself in a consultation with a millionaire widow he ran into at the Junction Stop. As soon as her husband kicked off she sold the farm and got millions of after-tax dollars. Not only is she rich, but according to Larry, she's *exquisite*, whatever that means, and since Larry's wife left him a number of years ago, he really hasn't had much going in the *exquisite* department.

When Klassen asks me why the *Winchester* was in the truck, I tell them how I picked it up at *the Reporter*, and how I got the shells at Woslewski's.

"So what's the latest on Jerry Harper?" I say when they're done with their questions.

Neither of them responds.

"Just stay out of this investigation, Bartowski," Klassen says. I remember the note on my steering wheel. It too used those words. Could Klassen have left that note? Is that why Fred showed up at the cemetery?

I find Larry and Rosie heavily engaged with the auditors. For some reason the Grays have an inordinate interest in the wedding, asking questions about the band, the hall and in particular the catering.

"Why the interest in our caterer?" I say. "To make sure she claims her tips?" I'm running out of patience.

Neither of them responds, which I take as the code of silence under which they conduct business.

After a few hours of painstaking examination of receipts with the Grays, we head down to the recreation centre to decorate the auditorium. With less than twenty-four hours to the wedding ceremony we're into the countdown, or meltdown in some cases. It being a green wedding doesn't help matters either.

We had to bring a lot of lichen, moss, sticks and stones from up north for the centrepieces, leading to no end of complaints from Rosie's mother. The invitations were printed on recycled paper, only real china and silverware would do, the ingredients are all organic, which almost doubled the price, including the locally grown baron of beef. The engagement ring is an official polar bear diamond from a Saskatchewan mine. Heck, they're even using biodegradable balloons.

Rosie is shelling out orders like candy on Halloween. Reverend Roy is flapping about looking for his copy of the vows that Annie and Randy wrote for the ceremony. He may be nervous because Enid is working behind the counter, preparing her kitchen for the main event. Roy glances in her direction. I guess to see if she's paying him any attention.

I notice she isn't. But she glances my way from time to time.

Annie and Randall come in carrying boxes of decorations, while Stu totes miles of extension cords and two giant disco balls. Behind them come Randall's parents, Andrew and Shirley McGregor.

"Hello, Bart," Andrew says. "This is going to be a grand event, don't you think?"

"I'm sure it will," I say, gritting my teeth.

"Hello, good to see you again," Shirley says. She's a strong woman. Probably has to be to deal with Andrew.

"Get the ladder, Bart," Rosie says, "we need the tall one to hang those disco balls."

Stu and I go out the back door to the storage shed. The hinges squeak loudly as the door swings open. The twenty-foot stepladder hangs lengthways on the wall. We each grab an end.

Back inside the decorating begins, Rosie and Annie doing a good impression of a TV design team, and we the willing workers.

While helping Annie with the decorations, I learn that she and Randall have found a place to live in Saskatoon. "It's a condo," Annie says. "Two bedrooms, two bathrooms. Randy can walk to work. I can stroll with Emma by the river."

When Randall was offered a third job by a Saskatoon firm, he swore up and down he wouldn't take it. But it turned out to be the best of the bunch, focusing on his specialty, and it's also the most money of the three. He and Annie discussed it and decided it was the best decision all around. Rosie is ecstatic.

"Is it a good neighbourhood for kids? I think you said you're planning to have three?"

Smiling, Annie says, "Yes, it's a good area and there are playgrounds and day cares right near by."

"Day cares?" I ask.

"Well, I intend to go to work eventually."

"Oh," I say, not really liking the idea of Emma in the

care of strangers.

In a few hours the auditorium is transformed. Shirley McGregor single-handedly set most of the tables, while Myra and Rosie's mom laid out the northern centrepieces and candelabra.

"The place looks marvellous," Reverend Roy says, having returned to retrieve his copy of the wedding vows that he misplaced again. After seeking Enid's attention all afternoon he finally gave up and left.

It's a cold night, not much above freezing, which reminds me the McGregor clan talked Randy into wearing a kilt at the ceremony. Actually quite a nice tartan with a burgundy stripe. Annie thinks it'll be "hot." I think it'll be cool.

On the way home, despite the temperature, Rosie is excited. "You look happy," I say, over the huff of the heater fan.

"I do?" she says.

"Yeah, your eyes are shining, you can't keep a smile off your face, and you're humming."

"I am not humming."

"Here comes the bride," I sing to remind her.

"Well, what mother wouldn't be humming? I'm so proud of those kids. Imagine having a baby, jobs, moving, a wedding *and* a murder all to contend with, and look how well they're handling it. They're much more mature than we were at that age."

I nod in agreement.

"So, what song are you singing?" she asks.

"Let's Forget About the Money," I sing in a lamenting twang.

Larry promised he would take care of the bar, top to bottom, so I finally relented. You gotta give him credit, he's willing to take on the big jobs, but I made him promise me he wouldn't drink. I just hope he doesn't blow it.

Now, all I have to do is wash and wax the car. I'll do that first thing in the morning.

The McGregors join us for supper. And we belatedly invited Reverend Roy, who had misplaced his car keys that we all searched for before he found them in his coat pocket. Rosie cooked two pots of cabbage rolls earlier. Now they just have to be heated up along with a bunch of roasted sausage and perogies—the trinity—served with a creamy cucumber salad.

The McGregors and Bartowskis sit together and join hands. Reverend Roy prays for a beautiful day and a wonderful wedding. And probably a date with Enid.

Andrew and Stu get to talking WWII airplanes while Shirley chats brightly as she and Rosie discuss wedding logistics. Turns out Shirley has oodles of experience owing to her work with the writers' festival in Moose Jaw. The Reverend rehearses the ceremony with Annie and Randall. They decided to forgo a rehearsal at the church, since the ceremony is very simple and involves only the three of them.

After supper Andrew and I retire to the living room.

"Help yourself to a drink," I say, pointing to a bottle of *Glenfiddich*—my one indulgence for the wedding. He pours himself three fingers.

"You know, Bart," he says, "I won't forget this money business. I appreciate you carrying the load for both of us."

I'm not sure how to respond. With my pent up anger, or in the spirit of the occasion. I choose the latter. "Well, Andrew, we have a nice wedding planned for the kids. And that's what counts."

He raises his glass in a toast. "To the kids," he says, and takes a deep swallow of his scotch. His already ruddy complexion blossoms even more.

"So, how's business?" I say, feeling not as charitable as I thought I was.

It isn't long before Shirley appears at the entrance to the living room, and says, "Let's go, Dear." She eyes his glass. "These people have a lot to do before the big day."

"Right you are," he says, polishing off his drink and getting up with a groan. "Bart," he turns to me, "it's been a pleasure to visit you and your family."

"You have a lovely home," Shirley says, "thank you for making us feel so welcome."

After wishing everyone goodnight, Rosie and I go straight to bed. I have to tell Stu to turn his radio down, and there's a bit of a kafuffle in the room that Myra and Rosie's mom are sharing. But soon things settle down.

At least until Emma decides it's her turn to be heard. Just before dropping off, instead of a picture of tomorrow's beautiful wedding in my mind, the note appears before me. *Don't fuck this up, Bartowski. Keep your nose out, or else.* Or else what?

Saturday, September 29ᵗʰ
Wedding Day

It's not a great day to get married, unless cold, windy and grey is your idea of great. The weatherman says it may improve later. Good luck, I think I just saw a snowflake. I turn up the thermostat and reach for an apron.

For breakfast I make bacon—regular and tofu—farm fresh scrambled eggs, thick slices of whole wheat toast and crisp fried potatoes.

"Morning, Daddy," Annie says, putting her arms around me and kissing me on the cheek. "Beautiful day, huh?"

I quash my gloomy outlook and say, "Lovely. You want some breakfast?"

"That's exactly what I was going to order. You got some herbal tea to go with that?"

I pour hot water into a teapot. "So, you ready for the big day?"

"Definitely," Annie says. "Let's face it, it's past due, right?"

"I'm proud of you today, Honey, and of Randall and Emma. You're a terrific family off on a great adventure. The best kind there is."

"We owe a lot to you and Mom," Annie says, "You're such good roll models for us."

"Seriously?"

"Yeah. You're never going to leave, and Mom's never going to stop loving you. And that's what I want."

"Well, if you want it, make it real in every word, thought and action."

"Look who's talking about action," Rosie says, coming in the door carrying what looks like a large picture frame wrapped in off-white recycled paper with a bow made out of dried cattails.

"What's that, Mom?" Annie says, excitedly.

"A toaster," Rosie says.

"Can I open it?"

"No. It'll have to wait 'till tomorrow like all the other gifts."

"We're off to get the flowers," Rosie's mom says, entering the kitchen with Myra in tow.

In addition to the northern lichen and sticks and stones, Annie chose to use tiger lilies, the brilliant orange floral emblem of the province, grown special for the wedding at the local nursery.

"I thought somebody was supposed to wash René's car," Myra says. As the wedding chauffeur she takes a professional interest. "It still looks like hell if you ask me. We have to decorate it too, remember."

"It's Daddy's job," Annie says.

"Figures," Myra says, stabbing me with a glance.

"I'm getting to it," I say, "right after breakfast."

Annie gives me a look that she borrowed from Rosie, warning and doubting at the same time.

"How's it going with the booze, Lar?" I say, perhaps to deflect the attention, but also to ensure he's got it together.

He sits at the kitchen table going over a list of figures and tapping numbers into his calculator. "Oh, yeah, got her all under control," he says. "I took inventory and replaced the lost booze." He holds up his list. "I'm going down right after the ceremony to set up."

"I'll come and help you unload," I say.

"Make sure there's enough," Myra says. "Nothing worse than running out of booze in the middle of a wedding." Myra's served her share of drinks too, having been a cocktail waitress for a number of years.

"Yeah, yeah, there'll be plenty," Larry says, an irritable tone in his voice. He taps more numbers into his calculator.

After everybody's had breakfast, I clear up the dishes and head out to look after the car. René graciously offered his Grand Marquis to use as the wedding car, so as Annie said, "We snapped it up."

When I reach the car, it appears to be sitting a little off kilter. And I soon discover why. The left rear tire is flatter than a pancake.

"Just what I need," I curse. I've got an hour and a half to get the car washed, waxed and shined and back to Myra. Then I have to shower and dress and be at the church to give the bride away. Pray to God there's a spare in the trunk.

Randy pulls in, helium-filled balloons jostle for space

in the back of his van. Emma's in there somewhere, laughing and batting at the multi-coloured orbs.

"Flat tire, eh," Randall says.

"Yeah. Hope there's a spare," I say, putting the key in the trunk lock.

Examining the spare is disheartening. It too is flat. I guess René never bothered to fill it.

"This is just terrific," I say.

"You can take the rental," Randall says, nodding toward his van.

"What about the balloons?" I say.

"No problem. Let me get Emma." He opens the side door to a smiling baby girl. Her eyes light up when she sees him. He unhooks her from the car seat and takes her in his arms. He handles her so tenderly, I can't help but mist up a bit.

At the Esso Station, Ernie is not there, and Lefty, his mechanic, keeps getting interrupted to serve gas. Full serve, you gotta love it. I notice Enid's mini-van parked at the side of the garage.

"What's the problem with that?" I say.

"No problem. She borrowed my pickup in exchange."

"What for?"

"Said she needed it to haul the barbecue over for the wedding supper."

I walk over to Enid's van. Inside are boxes and bags, cartons and crates, and next to them is a twenty-pound propane bottle, the type used on an outdoor barbecue.

"Has she ever borrowed your truck before?" I ask.

Lefty, who's finally working on my tire, grins and says, "You bet. And I remember exactly when too."

"When was that?"

"It was the day you found Morrison's body," he says, and grins some more.

I manage to lose a few more balloons getting the tire into and out of the van. By the time it's on and the car is washed and waxed—courtesy of *Fill and Wash,* the new place on the highway—it's a half hour to wedding bells.

When I get home Myra is standing on the curb looking pissed off. She wears a bolero jacket, a three-quarter length pleated skirt and boots. Her hair is pulled back in braids. She looks quite good, but her disposition hasn't improved a bit.

"Where the hell have you been?" she says.

"Flat tire," I say, as though it were an act of God.

She gives me a less than holy look. "We've got to decorate that car, you know?"

"I know," I say, making my way past her into the house.

"You're cutting things fine, as usual," Rosie says, as I enter the bedroom and start stripping off my clothes.

"I'm sorry I'm so late," I say, "but everything's under control now. Well, maybe not everything." I direct her attention to my rising flag.

"Bart, we don't have time for jokes right now."

"I'm so under appreciated around here," I say.

"I'll appreciate you when this thing is over."

"Is that a promise?" I say.

"Have a shower, you smell like burnt rubber."

After a shave, shower and shampoo, I slide into my new three-button, single-breasted black suit, a crisp white shirt and black silk tie.

Rosie's mother comes barging into our bedroom and pins a tiger lily boutonniere on my lapel. "You'll do," she says.

Rosie is more beautiful than ever. Her new hairstyle has turned from moppish to chic. She's wearing a dress that exhibits a hint of cleavage, and a black linen shawl that goes with her suede shoes and purse.

We turn to look at ourselves in the mirror and have to admit we clean up pretty good. Though I look a little rough around the edges, and the scruffy hair doesn't help.

At the church I hand Rosie and her mother off to Stuart. In his role as usher, he escorts them, one in each arm, to the front pew.

I wait outside for Annie. Of course it's the bride's prerogative to be late, which she is, so I'm left out in the cold along with a few stragglers, one of who is Chas. He trundles up the stairs wearing a suit with a black T-shirt underneath, his Mafia image now complete.

"Chas, what are you doing here?" I demand, despite his dangerous demeanor.

"I came to eyeball Kolchak," he says and goes inside.

Finally the bride arrives in her polished up, canary yellow chariot. Even the black vinyl top gleams. Orange tiger lilies pinned strategically along the hood and trunk give the car a magisterial grandeur as it slowly rolls to a stop in front of the church. Myra gets out of the driver's seat and opens Annie's door.

Annie is spectacular. Her satin dress outlines her fine figure, a full-length skirt floats just above the ground. She wears the wedding train that Rosie wore twenty-four years ago on our wedding day. Who knows? Maybe Emma will wear it one day. Annie carries a bouquet of tiger lilies with an array of dried prairie grasses.

"You ready, Honey?" I say to her.

"I'm ready," she says. Her wide smile proves it. And you can tell by the confident look in her eye that she knows what she's doing. After all she and Randall did try it out for a year. They know what they're in for.

The church is full and some folks stand in the back. Randall and Reverend Roy are waiting for us at the altar. We walk slowly and steadily down the aisle in time to John Lennon singing *Imagine.* Each pew has a small wreath of pine branches pinned to the aisle seat. When we reach the altar, Annie turns and gives me a tender, yet perfunctory kiss on the cheek. I feel a twinge of jealousy as she takes Randall's hand and lets go of mine.

Reverend Roy manages to find his copy of the vows

on the third try—left breast pocket—and in his reedy tenor does a good job on the heartfelt vows the kids wrote.

Tears stream down Rosie's cheeks as Randall slides the ring onto Annie's finger. I notice Randall's mom is also mopping up.

Once the rings are exchanged Reverend Roy declares, "With the power vested in me I now pronounce you, Randall McGregor and you, Annie Bartowski, to be husband and wife. You may kiss the bride," he concludes with a gleeful grin.

Randall takes Annie tenderly in his arms and kisses her. Rosie brings Emma to the front and all three embrace.

After the register has been signed, Reverend Roy announces, "Ladies and Gentlemen, I give you Mr. Randall and Ms Annie McGregor, and Emma McGregor."

Well that pretty much seals it, doesn't it? She's no longer Annie Bartowski, the button-nosed kid who could skate like the wind at age four, who broke hearts at sixteen, or even the woman who gave birth out of wedlock. That too I'm proud to say was Annie Bartowski. But henceforth what ever she does, she will do as Annie McGregor.

With the whiz kid on the organ playing a jazz version of *Here Comes the Bride*, Annie and Randall make their way toward the exit. We accept congratulations from our friends and family. Then we take pictures on the lawn. Mercifully the weather report panned out and it's turned sunny, calm and reasonably warm. I notice Annie shiver a little, however, and suggest we wrap it up. I wonder why Randall didn't notice.

In a convoy, we follow the wedding car blowing our horns unceasingly just to make sure that the whole town knows somebody got hitched. René and Stu are in the back of the van, both waving like the queen.

When we get home there's a message. The Crooked Lake Cat Cickers have lost their singer to strep throat. But for another hundred bucks they might be able to hire a vocalist from another town. I make an executive decision and tell them to go ahead. Then I hang up my suit and slip into some jeans and a wool sweater.

Down at the recreation centre I help Larry unload the booze from my truck, and the mix and ice from his car. He insists upon setting up the bar himself, so with nothing to do, I decide it's a good time to go out to the lake and check the airplane. On my way out I see the barbecue near the back door. It's large and it's hot, and the sound of an electric motor indicates that under the cover a spit is turning.

At White Pine Beach everything is quiet, except for the crows that keep up a constant tirade against the equally strident seagulls. Down at the dock, the airplane looks fine. I take the pump off the starboard strut and begin pumping out water that has seeped into the floats.

As I pump, a man wearing a toque and flapping parka arrives at the dock and hops out of a blue rubber dinghy powered by a ten horsepower motor. After tying the boat off he strolls up to the store without exchanging a glance with me.

Having emptied the floats, I meander down the dock to have a peak into the dinghy. There's not much in it, but I do notice what looks like the barrel of a small-calibre rifle sticking out of a nylon duffle bag. Toque and parka comes down from the café with a couple bags full of cans and junk food. Again he ignores me and loads into his dinghy. He fires up his motor and roars off, heading west.

There's something familiar about the guy. Then I remember what it is. He's one of the toughs that was sitting at Jerry Harper's table that day at the golf course. He's the one with the tattoo.

Without thinking about it for more than a moment, I reach for the ropes to untie the airplane. Soon I'm into pre-flight checks. The motor turns over nicely and I taxi out, taking off into the wind in the same direction as the blue dinghy.

And sure enough, I do see it on the north side of the lake. It's pulling up to a dock in a sparsely populated area. More importantly, I glimpse a red pick-up truck hidden from the road by a tall fence. And I'm damned sure it's Jerry Harper's red pickup.

I fly on by, as not to arouse suspicion, and then use my radio to contact the police.

When I get Hutt on the line, I say, "I think I know where Jerry Harper is. Over."

"Repeat that," Hutt growls through the static. "Over."

"I know where Jerry Harper is. Over."

"Where?"

"He's in a cabin on the north side of the lake, about a half-mile west of the golf course. There's a blue dinghy tied up to the dock and a red pickup in the back yard behind the fence. Over."

"How do you know all this? Over," Hutt says.

"It's what I see from up here. You'll have to check it out for yourself. Over."

Though my gas tanks are low, I stay aloft long enough to see police cars heading for the lake. A half hour later, with the plane secured to the dock once more, I head for home.

In the bedroom I hear the sound of scrabbling in the back of the closet. I'm thinking, what's Butch doing in there? But it's not Butch, it's Rosie.

"What are you doing back there?" I say.

"I lost an earring," she complains. "Without it the whole outfit is shot."

I'm not convinced of that, but I offer to help look.

Annie and Randall appear in the doorway, being tended to by Rosie's mom and Myra.

Randall has doffed his kilt in favour of the bottom

half of his suit. Everyone's pleased at how tall and handsome he looks.

"Nice outfit," I say to Myra, who's still wearing her chauffeur uniform.

"Thanks, Bart," she says, as though she were used to getting compliments from me.

"She's going to get a man tonight," Rosie's mom says. But it's clear Myra thinks her mom's dreaming.

As the entourage follows the bride and groom to the door, Stu says, "I want to go with you guys."

"Sorry, Stu," Annie says, "no can do."

"We'd like to have you with us, Stu," I say. "And we're picking up René."

Stu decides he's okay driving with us. I sense that he's figured out that with Annie married off and gone, he's top dog. Next to Butch, of course.

Rosie says, "I hope Enid can handle this. It's a big job, especially with that barbecue and all those dishes."

I'm still wondering about Enid. Why would she lie about the death of her father? And what about her relationship with Kolchak? Is there more to it than food? Chas seemed to think so. And what was she doing with Lefty's pickup truck on the day Lionel was murdered? But I can't talk about any of this with Rosie, so I say, "Don't worry about it, Honey. She's got the UCWA down there. They'll set her straight if anything comes up." I widen the search for the earring and find it under the bed. Handing it to Rosie, I say, "Besides, what's the worst that could happen?"

We hop into Rosie's van. It too has been spit and polished for the wedding, though I notice some of Butch's golden hair on the seats already.

Cars fill the parking lot at the recreation centre and line the street on both sides for two blocks.

Entering the auditorium, we admire the decorations, the candle-lit tables, and the convivial ambience. Most of the seats are already occupied and all of those sitting have drinks at hand.

Gail Harper and Jerry Junior sit with Dee Elliot and Nick and Wilma Taylor.

"Hello," I say to Gail, "so glad you came."

"Jerry's been picked up," she says. She doesn't look happy about it, though somewhat relieved.

I exchange glances with Dee. "I'm sure this is the best thing," I say.

"He didn't do it," Jerry Jr. says, looking at his mom.

Nick twists his head doubtfully, and takes a deep pull on his beer.

Dee calls me aside. "Jerry was in a cabin at the lake with a guy he knew in the joint."

I don't bother to describe my part in it. "So what now?" I ask.

"Who knows? Apparently he wants a lawyer."

Ernie Haidu from the Esso and his wife are here as is Lefty Holdner, the mechanic. Lefty nods toward Enid in the kitchen. "She came back as soon as you left." Enid can be seen slicing the baron of beef with a dangerous looking butcher knife. "Sounded real interested in what you were doing in her van."

"Did you tell her I was in her van?"

"No."

"I wasn't in her van."

Lefty just grins and reaches for his highball. I notice he's got several lined up in front of him. With drinkers like this, I hope Larry's got enough booze to last the night.

Mellow music with a rhythmic beat plays through the Cat Cickers' PA system creating a relaxed, yet lively atmosphere.

"You've got a beautiful daughter," Marg Woschuck, manager of the Junction Stop, says.

"She takes after her mother," I say.

The scent of gasoline overpowers Marg's perfume. Sure enough it's the gas jockey from the Junction Stop escorting her.

As I leave their table, I run into Reverend Roy who smiles benignly as I extricate myself from his weedy embrace. He mumbles something about psychedelic disco balls.

The guests are invited to take their seats for supper. After the Reverend's prayer, which is a bit wandering, members of the ladies' auxiliary fly about delivering hot plates to the two hundred and fifty jovial guests seated at the randomly arranged tables. The glass tinkling begins even before Annie and Randall begin to eat. Obligingly they interrupt their meal, get up, embrace and kiss for the insistent crowd.

Nick and Wilma Taylor are in the line up at the bar. Nick rolls his eyes at me. "What's going on here?" he says. "We been waitin' five minutes already. Where the hell's Larry?"

"Let me check it out," I say.

"I'll have a double rye," somebody says, as I make my way behind the bar. "Give me four beers," somebody else calls out.

When I get the line up down to a manageable length I go into the storage room for more glasses, and that's when I find Larry. He's sitting on a stack of beer cases talking on his cell phone.

"Larry," I say, "what's going on?"

"I'm on a break. I'll call you back, Dear," he says into the phone. I wonder if it's his millionaire widow.

"What the hell do you mean, on a break?"

"Bar service is closed during supper," he says. "There's plenty of wine on the tables, and non-alcoholic beverages are available. We'll be serving champagne soon too. It's only civilized, Bart."

"Yeah, but we got a line up out there, and they're thirsty."

"You tell those boors the bar is closed."

"Now come on, Larry, not everybody's as civilized as you."

"You asked me to take care of the bar from top to bottom. That's what I'm doing. Besides, why should we serve more booze than necessary?"

I can't argue with that. And I'm pleased to see that Larry appears to be stone cold sober. I go back out to the bar and face the music.

After serving a few last drinks, I close the bar for supper, ignoring the dirty looks from those left waiting in line. Instead my eyes wonder toward the kitchen.

As each course comes out, it's unanimous, the meal is superb. Well beyond the norm for these parts. "More like one of them fancy city restaurants," somebody says. The barbecued baron of beef is highly praised.

Wending my way through the tables I walk over to the counter where Enid is now cleaning her knife carefully. "Wonderful meal," I say to her, eyeing the blade.

"Thank you." She's wearing a boyish outfit with a long apron and chef's hat.

"I particularly liked the beef."

Now that I'm next to her, she looks at everything, but me.

"That's quite a barbecue out there. How do you hall that thing around?"

"Why do you ask?"

"I was just wondering."

"I borrowed Lefty's truck from the Esso garage, as I think you already know."

"Like you did on the day Lionel Morrison was murdered?" I say, watching for her reaction.

She doesn't reply, but I see a coldness in her eyes that wasn't there before.

"Why did you need the truck that day?"

She looks pensive, as though trying to remember.

"I was wondering something else," I say, unable to stop myself. "Did your dad die in a car accident? Or did he die of cancer?"

"What's your point?" Enid says.

"It's just a simple question."

She shrugs and slides the knife into a well-worn leather sheath.

"Hey, there's the chef," Jack Kolchak says, approaching the counter. Then he sees me. "Oh, hello, Bart."

"Kolchak."

"Can I get a drink?" he says, as though I'm going to get it for him.

"Sorry, Jack. Bar's closed."

He looks annoyed.

"I've got things to do, gentlemen," Enid says.

Both Kolchak and I back off, reacting to her official tone.

Enid's gaze lingers on me, as she fondles her sheathed knife.

As the Saskatoon berry pie and ice cream is being served, Rosie tugs on the sleeve of my jacket. "Enid's gone," she says.

"What do you mean, gone?"

"Nobody's seen her since you were over there talking to her. What did you say to her anyway?"

"Uh . . . nothing. Maybe she's in the washroom."

"No."

"Is her van still here?"

"I don't know."

I head out the back door to have a look. Her van is still parked right beside my truck. I go down the steps past the barbecue that's still warm, and look inside her van. And just as I do, I hear the shed door squeak, then feel the point of a very sharp blade against my throat.

"Let's take a drive," Enid rasps in my ear. She forces me toward my truck, holding the knife firmly to my neck and grasping my arm behind my back. "Get behind the wheel."

I do as she says. Having seen her wield that very long, sharp instrument on the baron of beef, I know she could cut my throat using very little effort and not more than a few of her carving skills.

I start the truck and just as we exit the parking lot, my rear view mirror reflects Rosie and Stuart watching from the back door of the hall.

"Drive to White Pine Beach," Enid says.

"What for?"

"Your airplane."

"What?"

"You heard me. Head for the lake."

What the hell is this? I wasn't planning on flying tonight, except maybe on the backside of a few drinks. The night is dark, there's no moon and the clouds have returned.

"I can't fly in these conditions," I say.

"You have a commercial license. You can fly by instruments."

"Yes, but you have to be able to see *something.*"

"You can see enough."

When we arrive at White Pine the airplane is securely tied to the dock, floating high in the water, owing to my pumping earlier today. And the depleted gas tanks.

"Where are we going?" I say, as we make our way onto the dock.

"I'll let you know," she says.

Once inside I check my dials, zeroing in on the gas gauge that shows both tanks near empty. We aren't going to get far, but for some reason I don't relay this information to her. Instead, I try to delay as much as possible, hoping somebody will stop us before we get off the water. But finally I'm forced to fire up the engine and taxi away from the dock.

The last thing I want is to be up in the air with this knife-wielding lunatic, so drastic action seems necessary. I extend my arm, as though to adjust the flaps, then hit her with a sharp elbow to the face. She cries out and blood spurts from her nose. The knife slips to the floor. When she bends to retrieve it, I crank the door handle and shove her out of the airplane. A splash tells me she's hit the water. I advance the throttle, leaving her behind. Thank God.

But a thump a moment later tells me she's still aboard. All at once she rips open the door, her face is covered in blood and she's wearing a look of pure rage. She thrusts the knife toward me, placing the tip on my heart and poking a hole through my new suit. I feel the blade against my bare skin.

"Okay," I say. "Okay."

"Now," Enid closes her door, "get this plane in the air, mother-fucker."

I'm not sure if this is the best time to tell her we don't have much gas.

The Cessna lifts off with very little effort and we're soon at five hundred feet and into the clouds where nobody can see us. With no flight plan, nobody knows where we're going. And flying below a thousand feet makes us undetectable by radar. So, we've pretty much disappeared.

"Where to?" I say over the din of the motor.

"Head north," Enid says. She cleans the blood off her face with a damp sleeve.

"Where are we going?" I say.

She looks out into the darkness, saying nothing.

I know we're not going to get far on the gas we've got in the tanks, so I decide to take a chance. I very slowly take the airplane into a wide arc, keeping us within a few miles of the lake in hopes it will be there when we need it.

"If you don't tell me where we're going, we're not going to get there," I say.

"How much gas do you have?" she asks.

And right on cue, the motor begins to sputter.

"What the hell's going on?" Enid says.

The motor spits and starts and finally stops. "We're out of gas." We are sailing along, borne only by the air moving over the wings. The silence is deafening as I watch the altimeter, scan for a break in the clouds, and pray for a place to put down.

"Oh, christ, we're going to die," Enid cries.

"It's possible," I say, somehow feeling okay about it. "We've got to find some water to land on."

"What are the odds?" She says.

"Not good," I answer, honestly.

"Okay, look," Enid says, "in case we don't make it . . ."

"Yeah?" I say.

"Just so you know," she takes a fortifying breath, "I never meant to kill Lionel Morrison."

"You killed him?"

"I didn't mean to," she says, insistently. "I just meant to scare him, and make the company admit its guilt." Tears appear in her round eyes. I'm not sure if they're for Morrison or her own imminent death.

The altimeter tells me I'm at eight hundred feet. I continue in a wide arc, flaps set at two notches to stay aloft as long as possible.

"I found out from Rosie that Lionel was going to be at your house that night. So I flagged him down, said I needed to get the tank to your place for the barbecue. He was more than happy to oblige. I had met him when I was catering for Sombrero, of course. He was a really nice man, that's what makes this so hard. When I told him the tank contained anhydrous ammonia, it was enough to persuade him to drive to the elevator. But when we got inside he tried to over power me. The spray gun was in my hand, my finger on the trigger. Before I knew what happened, he was lying on the ground screaming. I could see his skin freezing, his eyeballs disappearing. I couldn't stand it any longer, so in desperation I hit the hopper switch and a ton of wheat poured down on him." Enid's eyes flutter, tears fall from the lashes. "Before he died his hand broke through and he reached for the sky, as though grasping for something. Finally he stopped moving."

We've hit seven hundred feet and still no break in the clouds.

"What about Jerry Harper?" I say. "Was he involved?"

"No. Jerry Harper was just an easy target. It didn't take much to learn he had everything I needed and a bad reputation to boot."

"You put that family through hell, you know."

She doesn't respond.

Six hundred feet. Still nothing.

"Oh, god," Enid says with anguish. "I didn't mean for my life to end like this. I had plans. Big plans. Fuck. Now what? It's all over?"

"Hey," I shout, spotting some lights below us. "It may not be over." But we're no more than four hundred feet off the ground and there's still no water in sight.

But as we descend, a sparkling strip appears before us. It's got to be the lake. The closer we get, the surer I am, and then I realize we're right back where we started from. My circular strategy worked even better than I expected. That's the good news.

The bad news is I forget everything I learned at flying school about making a no-engine water landing. So, I guess I'll have to fly by the seat of my pants on this one.

The Cessna comes down to fifty feet, then twenty-five and what seems like an age later, bounces off the black water and goes into a steep rise. I push the wheel forward. Again we hit the hard surface, this time on one float. It feels like we're going over, but finally I'm able to straighten her out. When we come to a stop, we find ourselves in the silent darkness not fifty yards from the dock. I feel exhilarated and relieved, but most of all, grateful that we're down safely.

I'm not sure what Enid is feeling, because she's still in a big pickle. So am I for that matter.

After we float for a minute or two, I say, "So, what's this all about, Enid? Why'd you do it?"

"Do what?"

"Kill Morrison."

"I didn't."

"What do you mean? You just told me you killed him."

"Did I? There's no way to prove it. It's your word against mine." Her look suggests she might deny everything she said up until now.

"Yeah, I guess you're right."

"So, why don't you tell me the whole thing?"

"Why not?" Enid starts out as if she's told this story before. "My dad died of cancer. When he got sick the doctors traced his illness to years of exposure to farm chemicals. He used Sombrero the entire twenty-five years he was farming. And in the early days they had no safety precautions, and now many of those chemicals have proven to be toxic. Oh, we took them to court, but Sombrero refuted our claim, quoting studies denying everything. Even questioning the oncologist's reports. We fought them as hard as we could, but in the end they had more lawyers than we did."

"And now?" I say.

"Sometimes justice has to come from within."

"Anhydrous ammonia?" I say.

"The deadliest weapon in Sombrero's arsenal," Enid says.

"So you killed Lionel Morrison to get justice for your father?"

"It was an accident," she insists. "I just wanted the company to take responsibility for what it did. There's no goddamned way they should get away with killing people."

"Why at the elevator?"

She gives me an irritated look. "Where else?" she says. Then she sits thinking audibly.

"How did you manage to get the job with Sombrero?"

"When I found out that Morrison was going to be in Saskatoon, I *bumped* into Jack Kolchak on the golf course. He gave me the catering job with Sombrero. He checked out more than just my references too." She looks over at me defiantly. "He told me about their visit to your lodge and the Crooked Lake announcement, so I persuaded Rosie to hire me for the wedding."

All at once several police cars, lights flashing, come pouring over the hill and fly past the café down to the beach. Enid's eyes widen, but she makes no sound. We sit in silence for a few moments watching the activity on shore as though it has nothing to do with us.

Enid flips her streaked hair and says, "My mom left when I was fifteen. Took off with the hired man. I looked after my little brother and my dad for ten years. That's how I learned to cook and farm and golf. Everything I know, my dad taught me."

A minute later we are blinded by floodlights coming at us from two directions. I decide it's my chance to bail out. But Enid is not about to let me go. As I move, I feel the point of the blade on the back of my neck.

"Not so fast, Bart."

Through a bullhorn a voice says, "Turn on your radio."

I look over at Enid. She nods.

I press the button on the mouthpiece. "Yeah, go ahead. Over," I say.

"Ms Pond," I recognize the voice of Sgt. Hutt, "we don't want anyone to get hurt, including you. So what would it take for everybody to leave here unhurt? Over."

"Wouldn't you like to know?" Enid says, under her breath. Police lights strobe across her face and streaked hair.

"But please put the knife down first. Over."

I can feel the razor sharp blade pressed against my jugular vein and I'm sure its placement is no accident.

"Tell me what you need," Hutt says. "I want to help you get out of this. Over."

When she doesn't respond, Hutt says, "Turn yourself in, and this can all be over. Over."

"Turn the radio off," Enid says. She eases up on the knife. "Fuck," she growls, "I don't think I'm getting out of this."

After a long silence I say, sympathetically, "Maybe you should take what you can get out of it."

"Like what?"

"Media exposure," I say. "Tell the world that Lionel's death was an accident. Get the public on your side. Let people know about your father. Let them know that people like him are dying and why. You said some stories need to be told. Why not yours?"

Enid is quiet. Thinking.

Hutt's voice over the bullhorn summons us again.

I turn on the radio.

Enid looks at me and seems to make up her mind. "I want to talk to the press," she says. "And Bart stays with me until I'm done. Over." She now holds the knife blade against my back, right over my kidney. Again, likely no accident.

With apparent ease Hutt rounds up a national newspaper and a couple of TV networks, but allows only Dee Elliot to stand on the float and do the interview through the open door of the airplane.

Dee, who is broadcasting live to a global audience via the CBC News setup starts out a little stiffly, saying, "Enid Pond, can you tell me why you are holding Bart Bartowski hostage here in his floatplane on Crooked Lake, Saskatchewan, Canada?"

Enid's slender fingers stroke her swollen, but still perfect nose. "I'm not holding him hostage. He's free to leave anytime." The knife digs in a little deeper as she says this.

"What is it you want to say to the public?" Dee says.

"I want justice for my father. And for all the people who have been poisoned by Sombrero," she says.

"Tell us about your father," Dee says.

"He farmed his whole life using Sombrero chemicals. And died of multiple myaloma that medical experts proved was the result of breathing those chemicals."

"Ms Pond, are you in any way responsible for Lionel Morrison's death?"

Enid glances over at me.

"His death was an accident, I had no intention of harming him. I took him to the elevator to make a point. I intended to force the company to admit it was their products that killed my father."

"What happened?"

"I would rather not say at this time."

Enid answers a few more questions, before professing her innocence once again and submitting peacefully to the police.

Hutt and Klassen take her into custody, placing her in handcuffs and locking her in their station wagon.

After I fend off queries from the press, Hutt asks me a few questions then allows me to return to the wedding reception, with a promise that I'll come to the police station when it's over.

Meanwhile, back at the wedding, the police have put the festivities on hold—only non-alcoholic beverages are available—and no one is allowed to leave. The speeches were stretched, but the crowd has been sitting at their tables for almost two hours. The dinner wine— four bottles per table—was drained long ago.

The toast to the bride brings some relief as everyone is poured a glass of champagne. Mostly empty and half-empty glasses are raised when I make the toast.

"To the most wonderful daughter one could ever ask for," I proclaim. "May happiness follow you all the days of your life." I raise my glass of the thirty-dollar bubbly and say, joyfully, "To the bride."

"To the bride," the crowd echoes.

Annie is very gracious, thanking everyone and making apologies for the delay. She concludes by declaring the bar open.

A cheer goes up followed closely by tinkles to which Annie and Randall respond theatrically and smooch for a long time. The crowd hoots and hollers. Larry opens the bar, I catch his eye and give him the thumbs up. He smiles and puts his arm around the millionaire widow who's pitching in.

The Crooked Lake Cat Cickers take up their instruments. The strep throat singer has not been replaced, so volunteers are called for and Bill Bird is the first to take the stage. He surprises us with a growly version of *Five Long Years*, which is how long Bill's been retired, he informs us.

Fred Snell waves me over. "Hutt and Klassen are going to interview Enid," he says, "but they told me to remind you not to talk to the press, and that they want you available as soon as they're done with her."

"I know. I'll be here. And then, when I'm not here. I'll be there."

"Okay, as long as we know where you are."

"I'll be here, Fred. Or there," I say, tonelessly.

"You asshole," he says, grinning.

"How about a beer?" I say. "You must be thirsty."

"Well," he looks at his watch, "I am officially off duty, but I shouldn't be drinking in uniform."

"Don't worry, I'll take care of that."

I get Larry to set Fred up with cold beer in a teapot along with a dainty cup and saucer.

Jack Kolchak crosses the floor to where I stand as if he's about to ask me to dance. "Can I talk to you?" he says.

"On my daughter's wedding day I can't refuse any-one," I say, hunching my shoulders, *a la* don Corleone. Put a few drinks in me and . . .

"I'm glad it's over," Kolchak says. "It's better for everybody. The family, the company, and Lionel himself. As much as Lionel and I didn't see eye to eye on Sombrero's direction, I always respected the man."

"I'm glad to hear it," I say. I'm also glad Chas' suspicions about Kolchak proved false. I must admit, I too suspected Kolchak for a while. He kept turning up where I least expected him.

"And Enid gave you no clue?" I ask.

"Not a damn one," Kolchak says. "She played me like a fiddle."

Tara Spencer walks over carrying a highball and takes Kolchak's arm. "Hello, Bart," she says, raising her drink. "Congratulations."

Kolchak puts his arm around Tara's slim waist. I guess he's moved on already. They do make a smashing couple. Tara's silver-lame jacket covers a little black dress with a skirt no longer than absolutely necessary. Kolchak's suit is dressy and casual at the same time. Even I can recognize Armani.

"I guess you're glad this is over," I say to Kolchak.

"And you will have seen the last of me?" he says.

"There is that."

"Yeah, though I may come back to your lodge," he says, mock-punching me on the shoulder. "Now that I know the rules of the game."

"You'd be welcome as long as you follow them," I say, mock-punching him back.

People watch as the celebrated Tara Spencer and her handsome escort make their way toward the exit. I see Jack laughing with Charlie Mackenzie before he and Tara leave.

The lively crowd that remains dances on. I notice René eyeing a young lady of about seventy-five a few tables over.

"Why don't you go ask her to dance?" I say.

"I can't rightly tell what she looks like from here," René says.

"Does it matter? It's just a dance."

"A man's got his reputation to keep up, you know? Not to mention other things." He gives me an exaggerated wink.

"Well, despite all that, she looks like a cute young thing to me," I say. "Why didn't you wear your new glasses tonight?"

"Because you called me names when I wore them."

"I did not," I protest.

"I didn't want to look ridiculous at Annie's wedding. Them glasses," René says, "I got 'em off the TV. *Googley Eyes* they call them. Their ads talk like they can make a blind man see. And I believed it. But, turns out I was just fooling myself." René is quiet for a moment, then says, "I'm not sure if I should be driving anymore." He takes a healthy sip of his rye and shakes his head, regretfully. Then he gets up, goes over, and asks the cute young thing for a dance.

I notice Stu waltzing with Rosie, and Ron Diccum shambles by with Myra in tow. The site of big muscular Chas in a clinch with short, fat Helen Mousie brings a smile to my lips.

Roger Tweenes and Doc Chow come in after their hospital rounds. "So, heard you had some excitement over here," Doc Chow says.

I raise my eyebrows and say, "Where'd you hear that?"

"We had a couple of people suffering heart palpitations report in at emerg," he says.

"Congratulations on the wedding of those fine young people," Roger says, smiling. His white teeth are bright against his lustrous black skin. "In my country a marriage is really something to celebrate." Before moving on Roger hands me a card for another biopsy appointment.

I find Annie in conversation with Myra and Ron Diccum who seem to be getting along famously. Maybe her mom was right, this is Myra's night to score. But Ron Diccum?

"May the father of the bride have this dance?" I say to Annie.

"He certainly may, and it's about time," she says.

"I was a little busy, eh?"

Again she gives me a look she stole from Rosie, somewhere between love and something else.

"Is this all you hoped it would be?" I ask, as we sway

to avoid a gaggle of young girls doing a line dance.

"And more," Annie says. "Let's not forget about the father of the bride being abducted between courses."

Things wind down around two am. After dropping Rosie and Stu at home, I head down to the police station. The media surrounding the place is thick. As ordered, I make no comment to them as I walk in. The whole detachment seems to be on duty, despite the late hour. Even Netty Ostrovsky is at her desk. Hutt and Klassen, unlike myself, are full of vim and vigour, obviously energized by closing the big case. I'm surprised to see Mr. Gray sitting in one of the offices. Then I see Ms Gray. They both look very much at home.

"What are those auditors doing here?" I ask.

"That's none of your business," Klassen says.

"What have they got to do with this?" I insist.

"I told you . . ." Klassen says.

"We got some help from CISIS," Sgt. Hutt interrupts.

"CISIS?" I say. "The spy outfit?"

Hutt nods and raises his eyebrows.

"You mean they're not auditors?"

Hutt shakes his head. "They're intelligence agents. In a high profile international murder case like this they pull out all the stops."

"But why me?"

"They figured you would make good cover and possibly provide intelligence and access. We agreed."

"Access to who? " I say.

No reply.

"So you knew it was Enid, all along?"

Klassen looks over at Hutt, annoyed, as though he too had been left out of the loop. Maybe Dee's snitch was right, there was a suspect that not many knew about.

"What about the audit?" I ask.

"Well, there's the up side," Hutt says, "there is no audit."

"Is this legal?" I say, my fever rising.

Instead of answering, he offers me a cup of coffee, which I accept. Maybe a little caffeine will help calm me down.

"So, what did she tell you?" Hutt says. "We want to know everything Enid Pond said while you were with her in that airplane."

A couple of hours later, after I've told them everything she said to me at least three times, and they've exhausted their seemingly endless supply of questions, I'm allowed to go. On the way out Ms Gray stops me.

"Did Sgt. Hutt explain things to you?"

"Yeah," I say, not feeling very friendly.

"It had to be this way," she says.

"No it didn't. You could have told us who you were. It would have saved us a whole lot of grief."

"That's not how it works, I'm afraid," Ms Gray says. "Just like auditors, we too have a code of silence."

On the way out I'm forced to run the gauntlet of media that rings the entrance. "No comment," is what the police instructed me to say. So that's what I say.

Sunday
September 30th

The morning news presents the story in all its violent detail. Of course my exploits are chronicled in full. Everything but my CBC statement.

Despite that, breakfast is a festive affair. Charlie and Marlene who seldom make it to Crooked Lake brought a gift—elaborately beaded moose hide mitts and moccasins for Emma. The smoky smell pervades the house. Their twin baby boys are still sleeping off last night's adventure. Two small heads stick out of a sleeping bag on the living room floor where the whole family slept.

We have yet to hear from the bride and groom who spent their wedding night at an undisclosed lakeside B&B where they will enjoy breakfast in their suite followed by a couple's massage, whatever that is.

Rosie is bathing Emma, preparing her for yet another brand new day. Stuart is again gawking into the Sears Catalogue, flipping through page after page of guns. I still can't help wonder if maybe it's a good thing he didn't get the rifle. It feels strange to put a lethal weapon in the hands of a kid. Is it really necessary?

Around noon people begin to arrive for the gift opening and a little luncheon. Rosie has prepared dozens of bite-size sandwiches, veggies and dip, cakes and cookies, and visitors arrive with even more sweet and savoury goodies.

Annie and Randall take their place on two chairs in the living room. They open a card from the McGregors, then look around for the gift. Much clearing of throats and turned heads accompanies the fruitless search. I notice Andrew knocking back a scotch, as this goes on—my *Glenfiddich*, no doubt. Shirley manages to maintain her smile, though it's a little duller than usual.

The second gift is the painting Rosie did for the kids. It portrays Annie and Randall standing in a field of golden wheat with a deep blue sky behind them. Annie holds a bouquet of tiger lilies and Randall holds a smiling Emma.

From then on it's toasters and kettles and waffle irons, with the odd crock-pot thrown in for good measure.

TOX News bought an exclusive interview for my part in the capture of Enid Pond. I auctioned it off for some ridiculous amount of money. A windfall for our adopted African village, a pain in the neck for me. Tara Spencer looks extra good today, a snug fitting suit hugs her lithe body, and the makeup artist took five years off her age.

"How are you feeling, Bart?" she says, while a muscled soundman clips a microphone to my shirt collar. I can smell Tara's expensive perfume and the soundman's armpits.

"Are we recording?" I ask, looking around suspiciously.

Tara laughs.

"Okay, let's get started," I say, without adding, so I can get out of here.

The mobile studio is warm and not all that roomy. "We're here today with Bart Bartowski . . ." Tara looks seductively into the camera.

When that's done it's time for Rosie and I to prepare for our trip back to Stuart Lake where we have guests arriving at noon tomorrow. Rosie's mom and Myra graciously volunteered to do the clean up, and I also heard they invited Ron Diccum for supper tonight. I hope they know the Heimlich manoeuvre.

We load a week's worth of fresh linens, food and equipment into the plane, including my repaired thirty-thirty. Stu's *Winchester* is being held for evidence against Jerry, who was charged with assault, theft, resisting arrest and being in possession of a firearm, and in the company of another parolee. Fred thinks Jerry will end up back in the slammer for a while. I'm not sure if that's a good thing or a bad thing for Jerry Jr. and Gail.

Our flight north takes us over a patchwork of grain fields and a network of roads that devolve into green pine forests and the endless blue lakes of the Canadian Shield. When we put down on Stuart Lake, we do what we always do when we first arrive, stop for a few minutes and just look and listen. It never fails to provoke a sense of awe. Wilderness is good for the soul. And the air is ambrosia.

But my good humour is short lived as we climb the boardwalk and come across an unmistakable breach in the electric fence.

"Do you see that?" I say to Rosie.

Butch barks, having picked up a scent.

"I thought you fixed the fence," Rosie says.

"Over there," I say, forcefully.

"Well, let's go see what the damage is."

"Hold on," I say. "There could still be a bear in there."

I grab my 30-30 out of the airplane and load it with the special shells I bought at the hardware store.

"Okay, now," I say. "You stay here. Butch and I will go in and check it out."

Butch is pulling on his leash to get through the fence.

"Do you think that's a good idea?" Rosie says.

"Why not?"

"Because if there is a bear in there, isn't he going to come out through this hole in the fence?"

"Yeah, I guess you're right," I say.

"So, I'm going to go with you and the dog and the gun, okay?" She says this as if I were a child.

"Okay," I agree.

Rosie nods and rolls her eyes at the same time.

"Okay, Butch," I say, untying the leash, "you're on." Butch flies through the hole in the fence making a beeline for the back of the lodge—the kitchen area. We follow. A bear bellows and Butch barks. The full-grown black bear romps out through the hole in the fence, the dog in hot pursuit.

Once we get Butch under control we survey the damage. It appears that the bear was not successful in getting into either the kitchen or the storage shed, though there are claw marks where he tried to get through a window. Grateful, I immediately repair the fence and make sure the electric current is running full-strength.

Only then, with darkness falling, do we sit down to some supper left over from the wedding.

"You gotta admit Enid's a hell of good cook," I say, chewing on some barbecued baron of beef. But I can still feel the point of her knife against my heart and the blade across my throat.

"She seemed like a nice person," Rosie says. "Especially when she offered us such a good deal on the wedding."

"She offered you a deal? What kind of deal?"

"The kind of deal I couldn't refuse. A twenty-five percent discount."

"How come I never heard about it?"

"It was supposed to be a surprise." She looks at me through eyelashes and tousled curls. "Big surprise, eh?"

"She gave you a discount so she'd get the job and have an excuse to be in Crooked Lake," I say.

"I guess you're right. What do you think she'll get?"

"Well, some pretty serious offences. She could end

up spending a whole lot of time in jail."

After supper, we sit comfortably next to the fireplace. I've got my cup of tea, my feet are up, and there's no place I'd rather be at this moment than right where I am.

"Is that all you're going to do is sit around?" Rosie says.

"Rosie, what are you talking about? We can finally relax, can't we?"

She gives me an irritated look. "It's going to freeze tonight and I don't want to have the same trouble we had last year."

She doesn't need to remind me. A pipe burst and the entire lodge was flooded.

"That was some wedding you put on, Sweetheart," I say, trying to get her off the topic.

"It was pretty good, wasn't it?"

"It was spectacular, Darlin'."

"Except for one thing."

"Right."

"Well all I can say is, thank God it all turned out and you didn't get hurt.

"Yeah," I say. "And now everybody can get back to business as usual." Though I'm not sure if that's what people want. Morrison's death has stirred up a lot of controversy for the big agra-companies. In fact Randall's new job will put him head-to-head with the farm chemical industry.

Rosie shakes her head and says, "I still don't believe it. That woman was in our home with our children and grandchild."

"Let's forget about her," I say. "I have a little surprise for you."

"Oh, yeah?" She looks at me coyly, as if I'm about to give her a piece of jewellery, which I should be doing if I were any kind of husband at all.

"We got our lease," I say.

"Oh, Bart. Why didn't you tell me?"

"It's just one year, but it's better than nothing."

"I knew you could do it." She snuggles against me on the couch in the firelight, her warm body pressed against mine.

"You know, Rosie, you said you would *appreciate* me after this was all over."

"Is that how you remember it?"

"Uh-huh."

She slides into my lap. "I appreciate you," she whispers in my ear. "I appreciate everything about you. Especially this." She places her hand on my heart. "Let me show you how much I appreciate you," she says. Her hand slides down and she grasps my belt buckle.

We forget all about Enid, the frost, my prostate and even the wedding bill. At least for a little while.

TO ORDER

Visit
Red Tuque Books
www.redtuquebooks.ca

or

www.caronelpublishing.com